A SINGLE DROP

A SINGLE DROP

LARRY CUTTS

A SINGLE DROP

iUniverse books may be ordered through booksellers or by contacting:

iUniverse
1663 Liberty Drive
Bloomington, IN 47403
www.iuniverse.com
1-800-Authors (1-800-288-4677)

This is a work of fiction. All of the characters, names, incidents, organizations, and dialogue in this novel are either the products of the author's imagination or are used fictitiously.

ISBN: 978-1-5320-6587-3 (sc)
ISBN: 978-1-5320-6588-0 (e)

Library of Congress Control Number: 2019900036

Print information available on the last page.

iUniverse rev. date: 02/01/2019

*I hope you enjoy the book. If you do, pass it on to someone else. I
would appreciate any comments at: ASingleDrop01@gmail.com*

Thank you to all the family and friends who have helped me with the book.

*This is my first book. You can help me immensely if you send
in a review on the site where you bought the book.*

*If you enjoy this book, look for my next one, "Mysteries
in the Attic" hopefully coming out in 2020.*

CHAPTER 1

COMMENCEMENT

It was only a mild "pop" but all six secret agents surrounding the President grabbed their ears and fell unconscious to the floor. Their ear speakers had exploded in unison.

Sterling was now alone with the President of the United States in a locked room waiting for whoever killed the agents to break in and kill him. They certainly wouldn't want anyone left as a witness.

Drip - a single drop of blood fell from Sterling's nose directly onto the President's white cuffs, a nervous condition Sterling suffered since childhood.

Sterling was terrified. He started shaking all over like he did as a child when he went on bone chilling hunting trips on top of Parker Mountain with his Dad in late November.

Sterling was no hero. Being small in stature also made him look quite frail. He usually felt shy and avoided conflicts whenever possible. He would gladly let the President die if he could live. His plan was to roll over one of the fallen agents to their good side and take the remains of the exploded earpiece to hold in his ear; then play dead.

But the President was bold and courageous in character. His military experience kicked in as he quickly grabbed two of the agents' weapons. He tossed a 9mm to Sterling and told him harshly, "guard that door! Anyone comes in, shoot them. Aim for the head only; they'll be wearing vests."

Sterling meekly answered, "I've never shot a gun; I don't know how."

"Just point. Squeeze the trigger."

The President could see how frightened Sterling was and knew he needed a partner to help if they were going to survive this assault. Sterling was turning very pale. He needed to calm Sterling down.

"What's your name?" asked the President.

"Sterling Charles Russell the Third," he responded.

"That sounds more presidential than mine. We were meeting in recognition of your award for *Excellence in Accounting*, just before my speech to the graduating class, correct? I believe you had the highest GPA in this field."

"Yes."

"Well, given the current shape of our financial institutions and controls, you could do a lot to help our country in the future; but first we have to survive. Time is our friend. However they rigged the earpieces, my personal security guards have an entirely different radio frequency. Other agents on duty will not be affected. They'll call shortly for my detail to proceed with me to the stage. When they get no response, they'll come looking. We need to survive another ten minutes or so. I can count on you; right Sterling?"

"I'll do my best." Drip. Another drop of blood fell from his nose.

They moved the chairs and table to block the door. The table was made of solid red oak as were the chairs. They were both heavy and could offer some protection from small caliber bullets. Although the door was also solid wood it was pine. Neither the door nor walls would stop a bullet. These were not secure rooms, they were old college class rooms. The President knew if the assailants wanted, they could easily shoot up the room from outside. They must want to capture him alive, not kill him. But Sterling was a different issue. He was only a witness.

Knock. Knock. Knock.

"Please tell the President we're ready for him on stage."

"Which route bravo or tango?" The President answered, pretending to be an agent.

"Tango."

The President motioned for Sterling to duck behind the chair seat, then lifted his gun to head height.

Bang! "No such route as Tango!"

One round pierced the door hitting the man outside the door. He fell with a thud, slumping into a ball against the door. The President also dropped to the floor behind the turned over table next to the door.

Sterling was crouched behind a heavy wooden chair on its side and could see movement behind the door through the bullet hole. He aimed his gun at the hole. When he saw a reflection, he closed his eyes and fired.

Bang!

The gun fell from his hand. He missed the hole by six inches but must have hit the assailant. Blood was pooling under the door.

Multiple shots rang out. Bullets were entering the room through the door and walls. With a bright flash and a loud explosion, the door was torn in half. Wood darts flew everywhere, but the chair and table sheltered Sterling and the President. However, the President was pushed back violently as the table blocking the door was ejected by the force of the explosion. He was still conscious but just barely. Sterling could see how severely the President was shaken. Luckily, the heavy thick chair did protect Sterling from the blast.

Sterling picked up his weapon and reached it over the seat of his turned chair. Without ever aiming, he emptied the gun's magazine in the general direction of the doorway. Still terrified, and now out of bullets, he ducked his head between his arms.

More gun shots. More yelling, then an eerie silence.

"Mr. President are you hit?"

Knowing a familiar voice, "Agent Lavery?" asked the President in a weak and raspy voice.

"Yes."

"I'm OK. Just shaken up from the blast. I am not shot," answered the President.

The President knew Agent Lavery. He had been assigned to watch the President's daughter last year at the White House.

"Thank God you're OK," said Lavery.

"Yes, but also thank this hero – Sterling. It was only with his help I'm alive."

Sterling was still shaking but felt very honored by the President's remarks.

Drip.

CHAPTER 2

TWO YEARS LATER

The package sat unopened on Sterling's desk.

Click, click, click.

Knight to Queen's Bishop 3 (Nf3), check and mate. Sterling wins again, but unfortunately, he never gets to see his opponent's eyes of defeat. Sterling played chess almost every night on his computer. Tonight, he played Iwin, a regular every Tuesday night. The players all used alias handles. Iwin was a very good player but had never beaten Sterling. Sterling (handle Cmate), was very good at chess but not very good with people. Playing online was safe, neat, clean; no emotions; just logic and strategy.

Sterling powered off the computer and slowly closed his laptop. He carefully placed it inside its case and squarely placed the case on the desk. Everything had its place. Sterling believed that of people as well.

Sterling had larger worries tonight than his chess game. The package contained the final settlement papers from the divorce court. He neatly cut open the package, and could smell stale cigar odor as he removed the documents from the envelope.

Manny was the only woman in Sterling's life since his mother's murder last year. Manny and Sterling met in college and were married the fall of his senior year. To this day Sterling is unsure if she agreed to marry him because her parents expected it, or if there were true feelings of love.

Manny's parents were both dentists; well respected in their field and at the Andover Green's Country Club.

"Manny when's the date?" asked her mother. "Remember fall and spring are always booked early at the club. Sterling Charles Russell III would be a fine catch. He graduated top of his class at Bentley; already has a substantial offer at Fine, Fine and Ginsberg Accounting Firm and will probably have his CPA within a year."

"I'm just not sure Mom," said Manny. "I do have feelings for him, but how do you know if it's true love? How can you tell if he's the one for a lifetime?"

"No one knows for sure, so take some motherly advice. Go with your heart; but also, with your head. Remember the old saying, 'it is better to be a rich man's darling than a poor man's slave.' If it turns out that Sterling does not make you happy at least you will be financially ok. And; if he is 'the one' you have both; wealth and love."

"I'd love to meet his parents," said Valerie, Manny's mother. "I can just imagine what his parents are like.

Odd though, Sterling only speaks of his mother, never his father."

"I've asked him many times about his family in New Jersey," said Manny, "but he just goes quiet and cold. I know as little about them as you do; must be an accountant's nature to be closed mouth. Maybe we are wrong. Maybe they're poor immigrants," laughed Manny. "This air could all be a sham!"

"Someone paid for Bentley College and you can just tell a person's heritage by their presence. Sterling has presence," replied Valerie.

The warning signs were there but Manny unfortunately took her mother's advice and they were married a year later. The wedding was planned to the last detail. Manny was the visionary. She decided colors, themes, general ambience. However, it was Sterling that did the details. He selected every song for the band; every hors-d'oeuvre from the caterer; every arrangement from the florist; even wrote the best man's toast. Although Sterling invited ten from his side of the family, only his mother came, as his father was supposedly ill. Manny invited one hundred and fifty guests. One hundred and sixty-two came.

The wedding went smoothly and all to plan; except for a single hitch. During Sterling's first dance with Manny, his nose started to bleed, not a lot; just three drops. Thank goodness he turned his head in time that the drops missed Manny's white wedding gown.

To everyone at the wedding it was hardly noticed. A few that did see joked, "Hit her back." but to Sterling, it was terrible. A blemish on his wedding plans, an unforeseen unplanned for event. How could this have happened, he thought. In chess you can see moves ahead. A drop of blood from the nose is sudden and not planned.

Even today when asked about the wedding, the first comment from Sterling is about the nosebleed. Not about how beautiful Manny flowed in her gown; not about the fabulous five-piece band or great food; just the nose bleed.

The honeymoon was rough. Still a virgin; Sterling was both petrified and totally clueless in the bedroom. What should have been pleasurable exploration turned into embarrassment and avoidance.

To make matters worse, the resort did not live up to its brochure. Also, flights were late, taxis filthy, meals prepared poorly. Constantly Sterling was complaining to management about their standards. It sapped the joy out of their stay.

The honeymoon was a foreshadow of their marriage. His constant complaining also sapped the joy out of their union. The house was never clean enough; the food never prepared correctly; ... but the real stake in the heart of the marriage was Sterling's inability to trust and communicate with Manny. He could not share his past, about his family, or for that matter not even about their finances. Yes, as Val predicted, he did earn his CPA and advanced quickly in the firm and made a substantial income. Yet he also needed Manny's paycheck from the dentist office to pay the bills each month.

After 14 months, Manny finally gave up and hired a famous divorce attorney, Curt Stealheart, to handle the divorce. At least there were no children involved. Manny wanted a family, but Sterling could never accept the noise, clutter, diapers, general chaos associated with children.

Sterling read the court orders.

50% of all savings and investments

40% of all earnings as a payroll deduction

Their condominium with furnishings

Their Lexus

He was able to keep a few personal items and his precious laptop, all effective in eight weeks. The rulings continued but Sterling stopped reading. He wanted to stay focused on the large items first.

"I only have eight weeks to find a new place to live! Well at least 50% of 0 is still 0." Sterling said aloud with a large sigh.

"I need a plan; and a car; and an opportunity; or maybe just a gun?"

As any good accountant would, Sterling made a spreadsheet to better understand the impact of the court order and to help him manage the decisions he was now being forced to make.

Salary	80,000/yr.	
Less 40%	<32,000>	
Net Income	48,000/yr.	= $4,000/mo.

Monthly Expenses

1. Payroll Taxes (Social Security, Medicare, Federal Tax, State Tax)	<800>/mo.
2. Health & Life Insurance	<500>/mo.
3. Car Lease & Insurance	<600>/mo.
4. Rent	<1,500>/mo.
5. Utilities	<550>/mo.
6. Parking in Town	<400>/mo.
7. Food	<500>/mo.
8. Dry Cleaning	<400>/mo.
9. School Loans	<800>/mo.

Total expenses	$6050/mo.
Net income	$4000/mo.

Short	<$2050>/mo.
	CHECK!

Sterling was a successful accountant. He had helped dozens of clients sort through negative balance sheets. You start at the top and analyze each line. Much like chess, each category presents an opportunity, an asset and a liability. You develop plans to grow the assets and reduce the expenses.

He was good. He could do this.

Starting from the top – assets.

1. Pawn to Knight. Approach the boss for a raise in pay. Sterling knew he was valued at the firm and a small raise was not out of line. He just landed the C.T.B. account. That was a hard account to sell so the timing is good.

    potential increase $400/mo.

2. Payroll Taxes – Revise deductions

    potential savings $50/mo.

3. Stop all voluntary payroll deductions

    health care, life insurance Etc. $500/mo.

4. A car is necessary to perform the job, travel to clients etc. Swap to a less expensive model $100/mo.

5. Rent a studio flat with utilities $300/mo.

6. Parking in Town – Park further $100/mo. away

7. Food – Bad cook, eating in was not $ 0/mo. a good option

8. Dry Cleaning – Necessary for job but less often	$100/mo.
9. School Loans – Refinance	$300/mo.
	_____
Total Impact	$1850/mo. $2,050 - $1850
Still short!	= <$200>/mo.

Check.

Sterling was pleased with himself. He was still short but not by as much. There's always another move in chess; I've just not seen it yet; but it's there, thought Sterling. Sterling had a plan. There is an old saying, a goal without a plan is called a dream. Having a plan was very important to Sterling.

Sterling immediately went to work on the expense side. He changed his deductions, cancelled both health and life insurance.

Sterling did his homework, found a great deal on a leased Honda, and saved almost double from the Lexus. Sterling felt okay when he went to bed. The next morning was different.

"Mr. Fine needs to see you Sterling in his office at 10 am."

"Thank you, Ruth," said Sterling.

"I've seen the court order. We have to deduct 40% of your earnings plus $250/wk for your ex-wife's healthcare insurance," said Mr. Fine.

"What! What Health Care? The agreement said nothing about health care?" barked back Sterling.

Check

"Lower your voice," said Mr. Fine. "Remember to whom you are talking. I did not cause this situation. It means more paperwork for me. I'd like to add that the firm is in no position to offer you any additional salary."

Check

"Business has been soft and we all must make sacrifices."

Sterling had been on the waiting list at the Post Road Parking Garage over a year when a spot opened, he could lease. That lease was up next week so he could find a spot further out of town and save some money. In addition, the renewal would have gone up in price since last year. Nevertheless, that was not to be. All lots within walking distance of the firm were full with waiting lists of their own. He would have to drive to a commuter lot and ride the "T" to work. How he hated the thought, dirty, smelly station and cars, packed trolley's; street people ...

Check

Food – Budget at 100/wk is $16/day; in town!
Check

Refinance school loans – what if they won't let me. I can't default and work at the firm?

Check

His plan was quickly falling apart.

Ring.... Ring....

"Dad?.... Is that you? Hello—Anyone There?"

"Sterling I need your help, it's your father. I'm in trouble. I've been gambling and owe some dangerous people money. You must help me or they'll..."

"You heard him – bring me $5,000 by Friday and I'll let him live 1 more month."

Drip.

Check and Mate.

CHAPTER 3

HIS DAD

Sterling was very close to his mother, Lynn, and could have been to his father if it was not for the continuous string of family problems his gambling brought.

One of his earliest memories is of his father playing poker with his friends. They throw the pennies on the kitchen floor "for the sweeper". Sterling would pick up every penny the next morning; but he never swept.

At age seven, he saw his mother crying. "Mom, what's the matter?"

"Nothing, Sterling."

His father, JR as his friends called him, had just lost the food money again playing cards. JR worked at the docks as a loader. Even though his salary was good, the gambling took most of the paycheck. Cards, ponies, dogs, numbers, super bowl; you name it, JR played it.

"Johnny what's the spread on tonight's Celtics & Nets game?" JR asked his bookie.

"Celtics by 7," he responded.

"Good, put $100 on the Nets for me."

"I need cash first," said Johnny. "You already owe me over a grand. When do I see my money?"

"Right after the Nets hammer the Celtics. If they lose, I'll give you half my paycheck Friday."

"No; you'll give me all your paycheck Friday whether they win or lose! I'm tired of carrying this note. Pay it up or I'll send it to Ned. Your choice!"

Ned, nicknamed Ned the knees, was not a person to be in debt to, not for money, favors or anything else. Although a small man, he was ruthless. He would purchase notes from bookies for $.50 on the dollar and then collect at least double. One of his favorite methods was to break the kneecap of one of his mark's friend or relation, but not usually the mark himself.

Ned would allow his mark one week to pay double in full. If not paid, the amount doubled each week. Week three started the violence usually the mark's mother or wife. One hit on the kneecap with a baseball bat and the mark's life was changed. Their family was now informed; participants are ready to sell whatever was necessary to make the payment. No mark ever dared to go to the police. The few that did skip town were never heard from again. They just seemed to disappear.

But, the Celtics won, 112 to 96.

"JR don't forget my paycheck Friday," said Johnny.

"Wait; give me a chance to break even."

"Sure," said Johnny. "It's Wednesday. You have 2 days to get me my $1050 or I take your check this week and next week."

"Don't leave me with nothing. I have a family to feed. What do I tell Lynn when there's no paycheck?"

"Your problem. You deal with it," said Johnny.

"You'll get your money. Every last cent and I'll keep my paycheck too!" yelled an angry and enraged JR, as Johnny walked away.

JR had a friend, Tony, that worked the mechanical rabbit at the dog track. He had full access to all the grounds and knew most of the key people. Tony always said, "Dogs can't tell. Need to slow a few down – no problem. Amazing what the right mix of food will do."

"JR, this is Tony. I wanted to call you and let you know the fix is in, sixth race; Thursday, Zebra. Mortgage the homestead; this is the one we've both been waiting for."

"Thank you! Thank you! Thank you!" said JR. "This couldn't have come at a better time."

JR needed to raise a stake and do it quickly. The race is tomorrow, and all his savings and retirement were already gambled away, his charge cards all maxed. His car was barely running! The only idea he could come up with was to hock Lynn's jewelry. Specifically, a 5-diamond cross Lynn's mother had left to her. It should be worth a lot at the pawnshop. In addition, after he won, he could take it out of hock and Lynn would never know.

"JR what you got for me today?" said William the pawnbroker.

"Matter of fact I have an antique 5 stone diamond necklace worth at least $7000," said JR.

"Let me see man. Oh, so beautiful, so precious, I'll give you $400."

"What! Only $400!"

"Ya man $400."

"Make it $1000 and you have a deal."

"$500, take or leave it."

"I'll take it, but I'll be back tomorrow to get it back so don't hide it too well."

$500 was not enough. That wouldn't break even never mind put JR ahead. This was a sure shot, it had to be huge, besides it was a lock. He had inside information. The fix was in. Tony would never let him down. They were close even before JR saved Tony's life in Vietnam when he carried him on his back to base camp. JR even received a medal. Tony always felt a debt that could never be paid off to JR.

JR's only way left to raise money was to ask Ned himself. That was a line he was not ready to cross.

Thursday, 2 pm JR was at the track with $525. He sat and watched each race without placing a bet. The first race he picked Sarsaparilla. It won easily but paid little. It was the favorite. The 2nd race he picked EZ. Won again this time 13 to 1 odds. Could have made a bundle but stuck to his guns. Each dog he picked in the next three races came in either 1st or 2nd. He was so pumped, so excited when the sixth race approached.

The favorite dog was Rocko, but he would have picked Chaser, if it wasn't for his insider knowledge.

He watched the odds:

Rocko – 3:1

Cha-cha – 4:1

Chaser – 6:1

Zebra – 9:1

At the last minute he went to the window and placed his bets:

200 – Zebra to win

100 – Zebra/Chaser Quinella

100 – Zebra/Rocko Quinella

100 – Zebra/Rocko/Chaser Trifecta

25 – Chaser to Win

"There goes Yankee!" as the mechanical rabbit zooms past the dogs and the gates open.

"At the first turn it's Rocko, Chaser, Cha-cha, Zambie, Zebra," came from the announcer.

But, by the third turn things had changed. Zebra moved into first by 6 lengths! The real race was for 2nd place. Cha-cha and Chaser were in a dead heat. On the 4th turn Cha-cha swings wide, bumps Chaser into Rocko and all three stumble.

"NO! NO! NO!" screams JR from his seat. He saw over $10,000 disappear with the Quinella and Trifecta bets. His only winning ticket was $200 on Zebra. At nine to one that's $1800. After taxes $1450. $550 to get the necklace back; leaves only $900 to pay off Johnny. That's $150 short. So close. One more race could make the difference.

7th race $100 on Sunshine to Win.

Sunshine comes in 6th.

8th race $100 on Biscuit to Place.

Biscuit comes in 4th.

Final race $100 Bullet to show.

Bullet wins; show pays $150.

"If I'd only had more money today; if I'd borrowed from Ned; if, if, if."

Even though he left with $1300; $775 more than he came with, it wasn't enough to clear his debt with Johnny and get the necklace out of hock. He kept relenting – if only, if only... Even though he won, he still felt like a loser.

"Here's your money Johnny. Every last penny, just like I said."

"All right!" said Johnny. "Where'd you get this?"

"None of your business. We're clean," said JR.

JR cashed his check from the docks and with the remaining winnings took the necklace out of hock and put it back into the jewelry box.

JR felt better. He was out of debt and vowed not to gamble again. Again.

But Lynn was not happy when JR only gave her half the usual money for the house budget. She knew he'd been gambling again and told him so. "When will it stop? When do you put your family above gambling? When do you put me above gambling? When will you get help?"

The good feelings left quickly and so did JR– straight to the R&J pub. The more he drank the more he wanted to gamble. One big hit. He needed a stake to have ready the next time Tony called. Tony only called about every six months.

"If only that 4 dog hadn't bumped Chaser into Rocko or was it Rocko into Chaser?"

"Another Beer!"

Over the next few months, not much changed. JR kept gambling, kept losing more than winning. He was now into Johnny for over $3,000. Johnny sold the note to Ned!

"JR, Ned wants to talk to you. Get in the car," said two very large men.

After a short drive.

"JR JR, nice to see you. I knew someday we would meet. I bought your note from Johnny. $3160 to be exact. I want my money. Now!"

"Ned, I don't have it," said JR visibly shaking.

"Get it," said Ned.

"I can't. I have no way of getting it."

"Your problem," said Ned "borrow, steal, sell, deal, I don't care. Get my money."

"My rules are simple. Pay me $3,160 by the end of the week, we're even. Wait until next week, it doubles to $6,320. Wait one more week it triples to $9,480, and I break your wife's knee caps. Lynn, right? Works at the supermarket nights?"

JR was petrified, not just for himself, but also for Lynn.

"And, if you decide to leave town, I'll have you both killed. Talk to the police I'll also kill your entire family; everyone!"

Two weeks later.

"Looks like an execution; she was shot twice in the head. No exit wounds so probably a small caliber: 22 maybe?" reported Sargent Lyons.

Brushing aside the undergrowth carefully so as not disturb the crime scene of any evidence, "Was she raped?" questioned Detective Brown.

"Doesn't look like it. She is fully dressed, but her knee is very badly injured," answered Lyons.

"Watch your step on this jogging trail, it is full of roots. There she is under that brown shrub behind the rotted stump." said Lyons.

"Do we have an ID?" asked Brown.

"Yes; Lynn Russell; lives over in the highlands. No Wants or Warrants. No history of any problems, not even a speeding ticket. Married to a Sterling Charles Russell Jr. He has a file with multiple entries of drunkenness, bar fights and the like. A.K.A. JR. No current Wants or Warrants. All previous charges were dismissed or misdemeanors with no time served. No felony arrests on file. He works on the docks and has one son Sterling Charles Russell III that lives out of state," reported Sargent Lyons to Detective Brown.

"Was she robbed?", asked the Detective.

"Don't think so unless she fought with them and they shot her and just ran. She has over $100 in her belt pack and is still wearing a gold diamond cross necklace," answered the Sargent.

"You said them? How many?"

"At least two. We have two clear different boot-prints at the head of the trail leading to this spot. Forensics should be here soon and will make casts."

"Any witnesses?" asked Brown.

"Not directly. No one saw anything. The original call came in at 7:45 pm from that yellow house behind you. She reported a woman screaming, 'You son of a B. You leave him alone. I know you. I can pick you out of the books. You don't scare me. I'll...... AHHHHHHHH', followed be two popping sounds; then total silence." answered the Sargent.

"She said 'you leave HIM alone'?"

"Yes."

Bending down to inspect her knee Brown asked, "Did you find a bat? Looks like the M.O. of Ned the Knee. We need to scour the trails and brush for the weapon that injured her knee and the gun if it was tossed."

"Who Is Ned the Knee?" asked Sargent Lyons.

"He is a loan shark and bookie whose signature is using a bat on the knee of a close relation if the borrower is late paying his debt." answered Detective Brown.

Brown gathered his team together and laid out his plan.

"Sargent Lyons, the crime scene is secure. Good job. I want you to work with the Coroner and the

Forensic team. They will need help looking for the gun and weapon used to damage her knee. Get Precinct help to go door to door looking for any more witnesses. Even items heard, unusual people or cars could be important. I also want an officer stationed here for the next five days from 6 to 9 pm getting the ID and interviewing any joggers, walkers, bikers, that show up to use this trail. Have them also pay attention to their shoes. Note any in boots or not dressed appropriately for that trail. We all know it is not unusual for the murderer to return to the scene to see what the police are doing."

"Detective Tedesco, go to the local businesses and ask the same questions. Add to your interviews about possible cameras at the street and if they ever heard about Ned the bookie/loan shark. I will call you when I locate Russell and you can meet me there."

"I do not want to bring in Ned yet, at least until I can rule out the husband. Also, only use your cell phones, not the car radios. This murder is less than an hour old. Let's go. Move. Move."

The R&J pub catered to the dock workers. Rebuilt in the early 30's after prohibition ended, it retained much of the feel of that previous era. The long dark bar supported 15 brass stools. There were two dart boards, one uneven pool table and an old TV using rabbit ears, like it came from Mars. There were no windows. The lack of light helped hide the filth. Years of stains of all kinds, vomit, blood, and alcohol the most prevalent.

Showing his gold shield to the owner, "I'm Detective Brown. Is there a Sterling Russell here?"

"Ya. He's out back. I'll go get him." replied the owner.

"No, Wait. How long has he been in there?"

"The game usually starts about 4 pm. They get paid at the docks when they punch out at 3 pm and go to the bank to cash the check. They grab a beer while they wait for everyone to show. As soon as they are all here, the game starts."

"Really, they have been playing cards almost 5 hours?"

"Yes. The weekly game usually does not stop until about 1 am."

"Has Sterling left the building at all today?" asked Detective Brown.

"No. No-one leaves until they are either broke or I throw them out. What is this all about? Why all the questions?" asked the owner.

"Last question. Do you have a back exit?"

"Of course, but not from that room. Again, what is this about?"

Without answering the owner.

"Officer Williams, please stand by the front door. No one leaves. Officer Carol, please come with me," bellowed Detective Brown.

Bursting into the backroom. "Who's winning boys?" The room was so full of smoke; Detective Brown could hardly see. What he could see was over a dozen beer bottles, scattered food plates from the bar grill;

cash (almost all were quarters and just a few ones). and cards on the table; no poker chips. Importantly, no exit doors.

"Who are you? Get out. Get out now. This is a closed game. Table is full." The voice came from the smoke.

"I am Detective Brown, and this is Officer Carol. I do believe gambling is illegal in our fair state."

"Which of you is Mr. Russell?"

"I am, why?"

Again, without answering he ordered, "Officer Carol, please escort all other players to the front bar area. I want IDs confirmed. They are not to speak to one another. We will question each one individually once I am done with Mr. Russell."

"Yes sir," replied the Officer. "let's go. You heard the man. Everyone on a bar stool with an empty seat between."

"Mr. Russell. I understand you are usually called JR. Is that correct?" asked Brown.

"Yes. I prefer it." he answered.

"How are you doing today, winning or behind?"

"Actually, I am ahead about $50. It's a lucky day."

"JR tell me about these poker games. How often do you play? When do they start? Is it always the same players? Do you stop for supper? Do losers get angry? Anyone ever caught cheating?"

JR answered, "The gang plays every Friday after we get paid. Today is typical, we started about 4 this afternoon. It is the same five of us each week.

If someone is sick there is no replacements allowed. No one leaves until they are busted, or Jim throws us out. He even lets us use the back john. We each start with no more than $100, usually we have even less. Opening bet is a quarter with maximum round bet of one dollar. Also, no player can bet more than five-dollar total in an entire hand. It keeps the games civil. It is not worth getting angry, or cheating. Check with the others, they will tell you the same thing. We drink beers, eat some real food like burgers made of beef not veggies, complain about our wives, boss and work, and have a few laughs. How could this possibly be illegal?"

"JR, I am not here about the poker game. Today is not a lucky day. Your wife Lynn was murdered tonight on the jogging path that circles the pond at the park."

"What! Lynn was Murdered! Why? How? Who killed her? It makes no sense. Everyone loves Lynn. She didn't have an enemy in the world! No! It's not right." he shrieked. "Are you sure it is Lynn?"

"Yes. Come with me to the station and let's see if we can sort this out."

"No. Not now!" snapped JR.

"Yes now. That wasn't a request. We need to start with an ID at the morgue." As Detective Brown rose up from the table, he leaned in to an uncomfortable closeness and whispered, "just between you and me, how much did you owe Ned?"

JR went ash white. How could they know? Why would Ned kill Lynn? His mind was racing but he did not bite at Brown's tactic. After a long silence he answered, "Who is Ned? Did he kill my Lynn?"

While Detective Brown took JR to the morgue, Detective Tedesco interrogated the other players from the bar. They all consistently painted the same picture of the poker game. They all said JR was an addicted gambler that would play cards, dogs, horses, sports games, even numbers; but he would never hurt Lynn.

During the interrogation of JR at the station, no matter how hard they pushed, JR never admitted to any connection to Ned. JR stayed quiet and refused to answer any questions about Ned. He kept repeating, "I do not know who this Ned is, but if he killed Lynn, you better get him."

"It's not that simple," replied Detective Brown. "We have received confirmation from the Miami Police that Ned was, and still is, in Miami. We can only implicate Ned if one of his lieutenant's turns states evidence, and that's not likely."

Detective Tedesco chimed in, "We also have no useful evidence from the area. No weapons found. Nothing useful from other joggers, or neighbors, even the local merchant videos showed nothing of value. The only forensics we have are of the two boot prints, and the small caliber bullets that will be removed at the autopsy."

"We tell you all this because without your help, Ned will get away with your wife's murder. It is up to you Mr. Russell. For us to go any further with this case, you must fill in the missing parts. Why did Ned have

Lynn killed. How much did you owe him and for how long? Who are his hitmen that do his dirty work? How can we reach them?"

"Come on, give us something to work with." barked Brown.

"I wish I could, but I have no idea who this Ned is; sorry." JR was released, and the case is still open.

JR called his son Sterling and broke the terrible news.

The police knew that JR knew who killed his wife. However, JR held to his story that he knew no one that wanted to hurt his wife. His alibi was solid as he was playing cards when the police came to the R&J pub that night.

Although JR put on a brave front, he was scared witless: scared for his son Sterling, but mostly for himself. He knew Ned had Lynn killed and he knew Ned knew he knew! JR had to pay off Ned quickly and establish that he is not a threat to Ned, or he would be next. That would best be done with another bet.

JR processed his wife's life insurance papers the day the coroner released the death certificate. Very little was spent on the funeral. The casket was a grey canvas over pine and the service was only one day. Lynn's body was quickly cremated. It all happened so fast that most of Lynn's family could not make the service. They were outraged about the funeral. Even Sterling missed the beginning of the service, his own mother's.

At the end of the service, Sterling had another nosebleed, just a few drops, thankfully missing the casket.

Not knowing of the divorce, after the service JR handed Sterling the gold cross to give to Manny. JR knew how much it meant to Sterling and was feeling generous knowing how much he would receive from the life insurance. Sterling took the cross but never told anyone. He also never mentioned his divorce to his father. He did not want Manny ever wearing his mother's cross.

With some of the remaining life insurance, JR paid off Ned and placed a losing $1,000 bet to show Ned he had nothing to fear.

Sterling was devastated. He was very close to his mother. Sterling called her weekly and never missed a Mother's Day, or birthday. The card would always arrive exactly on the occasion date or at most 1 day early.

When he was growing up, Sterling and his mom spent most of the summer at the ocean. Every sunny day they would pack a lunch and just lay out in the sun. By the end of the summer, they were both a rich golden brown. Sterling always felt warm and good when he thought of those times.

Sterling's memories with his father were few except for the November hunting trips to the Parker Mountain range in southern New Hampshire. When Sterling was ten, his father would let him go with them hunting deer. Sterling would not hunt, but did enjoy the hours of walking trails, small roads, crossing brooks, and just the adventurous terrain in the forest. They would tent overnight at the top of either Evans or Parker Mountain. The views of Bow lake below were just "Awesome," to quote a ten-year-old Sterling. By age twelve he knew the woods and area as well as his Dad. That year they shot a small deer. Because of the gutting, Sterling never went again.

Sterling pushed the police to find her killer. They pushed back and told Sterling, "Ask your father who was responsible."

"What do you mean?" said Sterling to Detective Brown. "My father may have a gambling problem, but he'd never kill my mother!"

"Yeah, he probably didn't, but people he owes probably did. Ever hear of Ned the Knee?"

"No, who's that?" said Sterling.

"A loan shark that fits the M.O. that your father may have owed money."

"Ask your Dad. See what you can find out and let us know."

Sterling tried but to no avail. "Dad, who's Ned? Do you owe him money?"

"None of your business. You stay out of this. Go back to Boston. I don't owe money to Ned or anyone else. I'm going to R&J's."

Sterling returned to Boston with both a sadness for the loss of his mom, and pity for his father.

It was April before JR received the call from Tony that he'd been waiting for. "Hey JR; sorry about Lynn, I just couldn't go; I was too upset, I..."

"Tony, Tony, it's ok," cut in JR "half her relatives never made it either. It's ok."

"Tuesday, 3rd race, dog 5, Tree Stump. Just like last time, the fix is set. Bet it all to win... Bet the house."

"Thanks Tony," replied JR.

JR wasn't going to repeat the mistakes he made last time. Everything on Tree Stump to win, no quinellas, no trifectas to split the stake and this time the stake was going to be huge.

JR still had about $10,000 left from Lynn's life insurance but even that wasn't enough. His bookie Johnny would usually front a couple of thousand; but Ned was another story.

Ned agreed to $10,000 but, the same terms as last time. He also reminded JR, "Don't end up like Lynn."

As soon as the betting windows opened JR placed his bet $1,200 for Tree Stump to win. Back into another line $700 Tree Stump to win. He kept changing the bets and windows to not draw attention. A single $20,000 bet would automatically draw attention. As others saw the spread closing on the odds, they jumped on board and the odds closed to 5:1 by race time. That's still $100,000. JR felt great.

"There goes Yankee," calls the announcer. The bell rings, the gates open, out come the dogs like a bullet. That is all but Tree Stump. He slowly walks out in a daze; stumbles and falls over.

"Gone, it's all gone," cried JR. He went straight to his apartment and called Tony.

"Can I help you?" was the response.

"Where's Tony?" asked JR.

"He's not able to come to the phone; can I take a message? Who's calling?"

(In the background, JR could hear sirens), "No you can't. Put Tony on the phone now!"

"This is Special Agent Mackenzie of the FBI assigned to gaming law enforcement. Tony has been murdered. Do not hang up. I need your name and location to speak with you. If you hang up, you'll be charged with –"

Click.

THUMP! THUMP! THUMP!

Ned and his enforcers were at the front door. "It's pay up time JR. Gee I hope you didn't bet on Tree Stump," laughing aloud as he walked into the room.

"I like you JR," said Ned. "So, I'm going to give you a break. Would you like the break to be your right knee or left?"

"Ned – please don't!" screamed JR. "If you break my knee, I can't pay you back. I'll be in the hospital. I don't know how but I promise you I'll get you the money."

"You promise me – HA. Do you promise me that on your son's life also?"

"Keep him out of this. This is between you and me."

"Sterling; Fine, Fine & Ginsberg; Boston; wife Manny; how am I doing? I'll take that promise but I need a gesture of good faith first. Get your son on the phone."

"Sterling I need your help. It's your father. I'm in trouble. I've been gambling and owe some dangerous people money. You must help me or they'll—"

Ned grabbing the phone, "You heard him – Bring me $5,000 by Friday and I'll let him live one more month. Plenty of time for you to get me the $40,000, he'll owe me by then. Cash only. Bring it yourself."

CHAPTER 4

FINDING THE MONEY

Sterling thought back to when he and Manny were married. The dreams he had of their perfect life.

Sterling could visualize a large stone house sitting on top of a knoll in a large estate. Complete with tennis courts, indoor or outdoor pools, vast lawns and shrubs manicured to perfection by the live-in servants.

His garage was six bays, each with a classic automobile. The Rolls for special occasions; the Corvette for fun; the antique Hemi Cuda and the slower blue and white GTO convertible for the shows; the Mercedes for him and the BMW for Manny. The servant's van was parked in back out of sight from the road.

In his vision, the house was filled with beautiful art: paintings, statues, artifacts of every era. The rooms were set up to host large gatherings. An expansive entrance and foyer that opened into a larger vestibule complete with dual-arched stairways. A function room that comfortably sat a hundred and an immense kitchen attached. Game rooms, studies, computer facility and eight guest rooms each with wet bar and full bathrooms.

His summer home at Wildcat Mountain and his winter residence in the Keys; although smaller; just as particular.

The windows gleamed, the floors shined, the crystal sparkled, everything clean and neat, in its place; including Manny.

Chiffon Dress; hair always up; hosting ladies' brunch for the Historical Society.

Too bad he never shared his vision with Manny. She also liked nice things, but she also wanted children. That meant noise, toys, clutter.

That vision would have been nice, but the immediate concern is getting the money.

Sterling could only think of one way to quickly raise the money for his father. At the funeral, JR gave Sterling his mother's diamond cross. Although it was the most important keepsake he had of his mother; he saw no other way to raise the cash.

Sterling had a connection to Forest Hills Jewelers; he had been their accountant and knew the owner.

"Mr. Chapman, this is Sterling Russell from Fine, Fine and Ginsberg. May I have a word with you out back?"

"Sure, sure, come into my office."

"I have a problem that I thought you might be able to help with."

"Go on."

"I am in the process of going through a divorce and need cash. My wife is soaking me for everything. The one valuable I can sell is my mother's diamond cross. I just can't bear to see Manny wearing it. I thought; I was hoping you'd buy it and give me a fair price."

"Let me see it. Oh, it is beautiful. Flawless diamonds, wonderful craftsmanship. You do know that there is very little demand for an item as expensive as this. I would probably turn each stone into an engagement ring. The cross would be destroyed."

"I understand," said Sterling. "It breaks my heart, but I have little choice."

"I can give you $5,000 cash." Sterling felt his heart drop. It was worth much more than that. He looked around Chapman's office.

Chapman opened the safe door; diamonds, rings, gold and a stack of cash. Receipts on his desk for tens of thousands of dollars from jewelry brokers. Sterling did his books. He never reported any of these commissions. He was loaded; and here he was putting the pinch on Sterling. Sterling needed the money to save his father's life. Chapman was loaded. It wasn't fair.

There was a smaller window in the office that overlooked an alley. His feelings of anger kept rising. He wanted to push Chapman through the window with his offer.

"That's not enough. I need $7,000 at least."

"No. Too much. I can afford $5,500 not a single penny more. Agreed?"

"Agreed." Out of desperation.

However, Sterling felt angry; he had been seriously cheated and knew it.

Mr. Chapman reached to the stack of bills and counted out fifty-five crisp hundred-dollar bills. The stack only dropped half an inch.

There had to be $50,000 in cash in that old box, probably more, thought Sterling.

Sterling immediately drove to an arranged coffee shop in New Jersey and paid Ned the $5,000. Ned reminded him that he had twenty-eight days left to raise $40,000 or his father would join his mother. Sterling now understood who had killed his mother and why. Yet strangely, Sterling was not afraid of Ned. He knew at this time that he was only a pawn and Ned was a Castle. But, like in any chess game; a pawn can capture a castle given time, patience, and much thought.

Sterling drove straight back to Boston without saying a word to his dad before leaving.

Sterling knew many businessmen, bankers, and acquaintances through his accounting work. Unfortunately, he was not close to any. He was a professional, always kept his distance, always played by the rules. Everyone he approached for help said the same thing. "I'd like to help you, but I just can't at this time. Good luck. I hope it works out for you."

In chess, you can only cheat if your opponent is not studying the board. In addition, if he is not studying the board, you don't need to cheat to beat them. The game was almost over, and he was losing, losing everything. His assets, materials, acquaintances, were all depleted. He was in a corner with no escape in sight. A lonely pawn against Manny, the Queen; Mr. Fine the knight; Ned, the Castle. Even if he ran toward the opponent's side, Ned would catch him. He had to cheat; not play by the rules for once.

Sterling could not get Mr. Chapman out of his mind. He would instantly get angry even furious over the injustice. He deserved to lose. How arrogant. And, it would be so simple to just climb in that alley window and get to the safe. But how would he open it? Even as obviously old and outdated, it still would be a challenge for a pawn.

The more he gave it thought, the more it seemed to be possible; even deserved: money going from one crook to another. Both Ned and Chapman took advantage of people down in need, for their own gain.

Sterling thought, to do this, it must be done right; not 99%; 100% perfect. That also means:

-He could only rely on himself, no accomplices.

-No one else to make a mistake.

-No one else to worry about later drinking and bragging of their big score.

-No one to split the pot with. Just him and him alone.

--No one can get hurt.

-No guns to accidentally go off.

-No knives, ropes, clubs. Strictly stealth and cunning.

The perfect plan. Simple and detailed, timed, practiced, perfected, again and again. No room for error. Researched and studied. No physical evidence to link him to the crime. No financial evidence to link him to the jewelry store after.

Sterling's worst nightmare was to be caught and go to jail. Not just the loss of reputation, but also the thought of living in a cell with who knows what for a cellmate, the stench, the germs, the filth. The thought was so stomach turning he would see his Dad fall into Ned's hands first if need be.

Drip. Sterling could absolutely not be caught.

CHAPTER 5

THE PLAN

Sterling drafted an overall plan, nothing on paper; strictly committed to memory.

Using his accounting skills, he would convince Chapman of a likely surprise government audit. Given Chapman's not reported profits, he would want to clean up and tighten his affairs. This would allow Sterling access to all his records and equally important, access to the backroom where the records are stored.

Sterling could plant a hidden video camera and find out the safe's combination. The alley to the building would be easy. The alley was cluttered with dumpsters and trash. A rainy night would be best. He would also need an alibi.

"Hello Mr. Chapman. This is Sterling Russell from Fine, Fine, and Ginsberg. I have noticed a general trend by the Federal auditors of doing surprise audits of independent jewelers. Apparently, they have been successful recovering large sums of moneys for unreported profits; mostly from Nigerian diamond brokers."

"With your permission, I would like to do an internal audit first to make sure you will have no problem. You helped me out by purchasing my mom's cross, so this is a way for me to repay you. I can do the audit partly from the firm and the rest I'll do on my own time, no charge, should take about a week."

"Do you really think this is necessary?" asked Mr. Chapman.

"Well I'm reading the cover story in *Accounting Real* our monthly trade journal, and it explains the Fed's focus and why...I think it's a good idea; but it's your call. You decide."

"Sterling; if you do this; what would you need from me?"

"Basically, access to your financial records and a place to work."

"Ok. When?"

"I'll start tomorrow afternoon."

"Thank you, Sterling, for the tip, I appreciate the heads up; but skip a day. I have a few things to organize before you come."

Sterling knew that was Chapman's window to get rid of the unreported commissions.

Sterling knew that he would be the obvious suspect by both the police and Chapman, too much of a coincidence, auditor in back room, then burglary. Sterling was lucky. He had researched the web from the library, to find an article linking audits to jewelry stores. He casually left the issue on the bottom of a neat stack of trade journals on his coffee table.

By working in the jewelry store's back room office his fingerprints, DNA, hair, etc. are to be expected if found by the police; but not in the alley; or by the window or safe. Sterling usually wore his hair on the shorter side: neat and trim. He had his barber go very close this time. There would be no need for another hair cut before the job. No loose clippings to fall out in the wrong place to later be found by the police. He had his eyebrows and nose hair trimmed also.

Over the years, he had watched almost every episode of CSI. He knew how thorough the crime lab could be in finding physical evidence. Sterling wanted to make sure there would be none to be found.

Sterling set up a Dump Bag. It was just a plastic trash bag, but one set up to quickly collect any possible evidence for disposal. Sterling purchased double of anything that may be found but from another source. He purchased a generic brand of hairspray. He would spray his hair, so it would stick together, then ditch the can into the Dump Bag. After the job he would shower and spray on his own high-end brand, Ultimen. Even if they find the spray it won't match his.

He paid cash for black tee shirts at a second-hand outlet along with a pair of Jeans. Nothing like the high-quality clothing he usually wears. He also bought cheap sneakers, and a black baseball cap. If anything was torn or caught there would be no trace to him. All Sterling had to do was get rid of the single Dump Bag.

He thought first to burn it, but where? Smoke and fire would cause notice. Sometimes the best place to hide something is in plain view. As long as he selected the trash pickup day to do the heist; he could drop the bag before dawn on the curbside. Any house with a large pile of trash bags would do.

At the jewelry store, the webcam worked well except it was not able to read the numbers. The safe was so old you could barely see them. Sterling spilt a small amount of white out down the front of the safe and onto the dial at number 10. From reviewing the tape repeatedly, he could determine the numbers {left twice to 55, right once to 16, left to 9}.

Sterling took the web cam, placed it in a shopping bag, and smashed it with his hammer, then emptied that bag into the, Dump Bag. He had purchased the camera and an auto dial phone system used, from the Kaig's List online. Cash only, no trace.

The phone system would provide his alibi. When asked by the police, where were you; he would answer that, "I was making calls to my clients. Terrible night though. I worked on the account most of the evening. When I called the clients, I just got their answering machines. I have no way to prove this though; I just hung up and didn't leave a message." Sterling knew they could verify via the phone records.

Sterling knew which of his accounts would be at their annual FMB convention in Chicago. It's great being an accountant. The records at the jewelry store also showed that the stores alarm system was installed in 1962. It included an interior siren only, no external connection to a service, to the police, or even an outside bell.

Sterling watched Chapman alarm the system twice. When it was armed, the siren in the ceiling chirped once to indicate it was set. The horn was located directly above the door. Slide the egg grate ceiling tile back and cut the wire from the battery. Simple; and the best part; to allow the store owner time to leave (or enter) once alarmed; there is a 30 second delay before the horn blows, plenty of time to snip a wire. Lastly break a clock at the store so the police can establish the time.

To finish his alibi, as soon as the job is done; call the building super to fix the toilet in his apartment. Scatter work papers on the tables so he can testify that Sterling was working at home. A simple disconnect of the handle chain using gloves that go into the Dump Bag.

Sterling secured three lockers at the bus terminal, a good place to hide the money and jewelry. Mr. Chapman was old. Hopefully, he would have died before Sterling sold any of the jewelry; though he was hoping to find his mother's cross intact. He knew the jewelry was traceable. That could only be sold if desperate.

The money was another matter. He needed the cash to pay off Ned completely; hopefully, there was enough in the safe. If there was more; that also had to be stashed away for many years, used infrequently to not cause suspicion.

He made the plan quickly. He had to, soon he would lose the apartment to Manny. It had to work. It had to be perfect, no mistakes. Sterling went over the plan again and again in his mind.

7:00 p.m. Dress,

- Wrap in plastic wrap, rubber gloves
- Use alternate clothing
- Spray hair lightly

7:15 Drive to School Street and park,

- Walk to alley, keep hands in pockets

7:30 Break small office window,

- Clip wires to alarm
- Open safe
- Pack bag
- Break clock
- Out the window

7:30 At home, machines,

- Auto dial calls client's answering machine

7:45 Drop off money and jewelry to bus lockers,

- Count out just enough to give Ned and bundle
- Leave Jewelry in one locker

- Cash for Ned in a second locker
- Any other cash in a 3rd

8:00 Drive to house,

- Swap phones
- Auto dial to Dump Bag
- Shower and change; clothes to Dump Bag.

8:10 Put out 1 trash bag as usual,

- Put Dump Bag out at neighbors for early pickup
- Knock on superintendent's door —ask him to fix the toilet

Most importantly – life now goes on as normal. Pretend none of this happened.

It could work. It must work. It was low risk. No one could get hurt. It's not likely he would be caught. No one else to rely on. Neat, tidy and well planned, like a chess game.

Oh God; please don't let me go to jail!

Drip.

CHAPTER 6

———— ◆►◆ ————

THE HEIST

The perfect night; dark, windy, and raining. No one would be out. It was as raw and cold as being at the Boston docks during a Northeaster in November.

7:00 pm Sterling was wrapping his body in wrap.

He was about half done when the doorbell rang.

"Mr. Russell, you there?"

"Who is it?" said Sterling.

"It's Ted the super."

Sterling's heart dropped. The plan had not even started and there is already a hitch.

"What do you want?" asked Sterling.

"Had complaints of no heat upstairs. Is yours working ok?"

"Yeah. No problem."

"Thanks."

Sterling thought after that this could just reinforce his alibi.

7:15 to the car; to School Street and park. Deserted. Perfect. No one out. Walk to alley window and break pane

The 30 seconds starts now....

29   turn the latch

28   open the window

27   climb up

26   clear out glass with flashlight

25   squeeze through

24

23

22

21   turn on flashlight

20   walks to front door

19

18

17   move chair in front

16   step up

15   move ceiling tile

14

13

12   find wire

11

10

9

8   get cutters

7

6

5   clip – plenty of time

Chair back.

To the safe.

Sterling's heart was pounding. He thought it might explode. He never felt so nervous since the Presidential shootout. His hands were shaking so much he could not turn the dial on the safe.

He kept saying to himself – calm down, breath; he deserves it; easy, pawn to his Bishop.

His hands stopped shaking. Sterling spun the dial, turned the handle and nothing! The safe wouldn't open! 55, 16, 9, LRL. No; RLR No. It took ten minutes of adjusting numbers before it opened with 57, 18, 11. It may have been an old safe; but it was very precise. It was the longest ten minutes of Sterling's life.

The door opened, and it was all there. The stack of mixed bills, mostly Hundreds; a small cloth bag with a wire pull string that was sealed with a lead clamp like the old lead weights used in fishing. The bag was not heavy. Sterling thought it must be jewelry and expensive jewelry given how it was sealed.

Most importantly, his mother's cross; untouched.

No time to look in the bag or check the money, Sterling immediately went to the workbench where he selected a new anniversary clock. Sterling knocked it onto the floor. It stopped ticking.

Out the window to the car. Gloves off. Money for Ned put into 1 envelope, the remaining money and his mother's cross in a second. The small black bag stood alone.

To the bus terminal where each was given its own locker. The time 7:50. Perfect. Almost over.

Back to the apartment. Quick Shower. Wire cutters, gloves, clothes, wrap, phone calling machine; all to the Dump Bag and out to the street. Huge piles of rubbish across the street. One more bag will never be noticed; and it will be gone by sunrise.

Knock, knock. "Ted; this is Sterling from unit 19. My toilet's broken can you help?"

"Sure. No problem."

Exactly as planned; Ted observed the paper cluttered table, "Working hard I see. Don't you ever relax?"

"I was just reviewing a few clients' quarterly reports," replied Sterling. "It's sometimes easier to call them in the evening."

"Oh, the chain just fell off the handle; a two second fix."

"Thanks."

"Hey," said Ted, "How'd you cut your hand?"

Sterling went pale and almost passed out. He didn't cut his hand, or did he? His mind went fuzzy, his skin clammy and moist.

With a quick wipe it was gone. "I didn't. Don't know what that was. Wasn't blood."

"Good night."

"Good night, Ted."

But it was blood. He looked at the tissue again. It was blood. He flushed the tissue. How? When? He checked over his skin. No cuts, no blood?

Then he saw his nose in the bathroom mirror. He had a drop of blood from his nose. When did it happen? More important, where did it happen?

How could this happen? The perfect plan spoiled by a single drop of blood, just like his wedding and look how that turned out he thought. One drop is all that the lab would need to prove DNA. Was it by the front door? The safe? The work bench? The window? Did it happen in the apartment? Was there only 1 drop or was there more? Was the only drop the one on his hand?

His mind was racing:

Think; think; what do I do now! His thoughts were random and that frightened Sterling immensely. He was used to order.

I need a story ready for the police if they find my blood. I'll tell them I cut myself last week. No, no, if I did, I'd have a scar not yet healed.

I could cut myself with a knife and make a scare but is nose blood different? Does it contain mucus? Can they tell the age of blood?

I'll just tell them I don't know. They'll never believe that....

Do I have a cut from the window glass? In my hair? Maybe they won't find it? – No, it came from my nose!

Sterling kept going over and over in his mind all night, where and what to say if asked by the police.

He was awake all night in his self-torture. The perfect plan wrecked by a single drop of blood. It wasn't fair.

At dawn he finally dozed off only to be rattled out of bed by a Bam! Bam! Bam! on the front door.

"Police; Open the door! We have a search warrant."

CHAPTER 7

THE WARRANT

With less than an hour of sleep, his mind was as foggy as Boston Harbor. He knew he would be a suspect but not this fast.

"Ok, ok," he yelled back. "I'll be right there."

As he opened the door, six police entered quickly. The four uniformed officers walked past him each going different ways. The two in suits stopped in front of Sterling.

"Sterling Russell?"

"Yes."

Handing him the search warrant; "This gives us the authority to search your apartment and car for merchandise stolen from Forest Hills Jewelry store. Although you are not under arrest at this time, I would like to advise you that you are a suspect in this crime and anything that you say can and will be used against you in a court of law. You have the right to an attorney present at questioning and if you cannot afford one, one will be appointed by the court."

"Mr. Russell, do you understand these rights?"

"Yes."

"But why am I a suspect?"

"We'll ask the questions here," barked back Detective O'Brien. "Let's go to the station and have a nice long chat." Sterling's mind was starting to clear. He wanted to make sure they found the work papers on the table to establish his alibi.

"When was it robbed?"

"Last night," said the other Detective, Scott. "Where were you last night?"

"Here."

"All night?"

"Yes," said Sterling.

"Can you prove that?" asked O'Brien. "Was anyone with you?"

"Well, I spoke to the landlord a little after 7 pm about the heat system."

"In person or on the phone?" asked Scott.

"Kind of in person," said Sterling.

"This is nonsense; give me the cuffs. Let's go to our house," said O'Brien. "You want to give us flip answers."

"No! No! Wait. I was in the living room reading over these journals (pointing to the coffee table). He yelled through the door and I answered him. His name is Ted. Check with him."

"Don't worry we will."

"He also fixed my toilet sometime between 8:30-9:00. It would not flush. He saw me then."

"Look at my table. I was working on clients. I even made calls to 2 of them."

O'Brien interrupting – "We'll need names and numbers to confirm your story."

"I'll gladly give them to you, but it won't matter. Neither of them were at home. I got answering machines; but I did not leave any messages. I just hung up."

"Shortly after, I went to bed. I cannot prove anything after Ted left until you came. You just have to believe me."

"Why am I a suspect?"

"Were you Chapman's accountant?"

"Yes."

"Did you just spend over a week in his backroom?"

"Yes."

"Did you see his safe open?"

"Yes, once."

"Are you in financial need?"

"Yes – my wife is divorcing me. If you want to check the car, do it quickly or it will be her car you'll be checking."

Detective Scott coming back from the property owner; "his story checks out."

"Mr. Russell; did you ever leave your apartment last night?"

"No."

"You're sure."

"Yes."

"Oh wait; I did put a bag of trash out. That's probably gone; we have an early pick up."

Sterling glanced out the window and could not believe his eyes. The piles of trash were still there, including the neighbor's huge pile of green trash bags topped by a single black bag!

Then it hit him, holiday week. Trash is picked up one day later.

His stomach sank. He went pale. He was sure to go to jail if they found it.

"Mr. Russell, how many bags did you put out?"

"Only one."

"What color bag, black like the one in this barrel?"

"Yes."

"Let's go, show me and bring your car keys. Your car will be impounded for a while."

Sterling went to the street and pulled off his one black house bag. Detective O'Brien told the police officer "to open every bag from this apartment complex."

Thirty feet away across the street sat all the proof to put Sterling away for a long, long time.

Sterling kept thinking about jail, the smell; the inmates, the disgust, the illiterate; the guards. He felt sick.

The rest of the police officers came out and said nothing.

"Ok. Mr. Russell," said O'Brien, "we are done, but stay close; don't leave town."

"That's a problem detective. I sometimes must travel for work. I am an accountant. My reputation is everything. I can't tell a client I can't go to his office because the police are investigating me!"

"Also, my dad in N.J. is sick and I need to see him. I would be glad to give you names, times, and addresses before I go. Please. I have cooperated with you. I've done nothing wrong; I don't need to run."

Sterling kept seeing the black bag over the detective's right shoulder as he spoke.

"You're the perfect flight suspect. Broke; going through a divorce; no family close," said O'Brien.

"Except one thing, I have a great job and one very hard to get. I work at one of the top accounting firms in Boston. I've worked years to get here. That is why I would not run even if I were a suspect. Oh, and did I mention, I did nothing wrong."

"Interesting choice of words," noted Scott.

"Not that you're not guilty, that 'you did nothing wrong'. Did Chapman owe you anything? Separate accounting books maybe? Did he stiff you on some jewelry?"

"Enough— Either arrest me or get out. I told you I'm going to see my dad in N.J.; and I'll visit clients as usual in state. If I go out of state other than that, I will call you. Ok?"

"Yeah. See you soon," said O'Brien.

"Hit a nerve, did we?" said Scott.

Sterling knew from the tone that getting the money from the bus terminal would be much harder than he thought. He knew the police would be watching him, but for how long? Best thing is to work as usual and wait it out as long as possible. Nevertheless, deadlines were fast approaching; finding a new apartment; car; with Ned the Knee.

Why did they find out about the theft so quickly? They had time to get a warrant and be here so early; someone must have reported it very early. Did that someone see him? Was there a witness? Was there physical evidence that connected him to the crime? Why was he so quickly fingered as a suspect? Enough to convince a judge to issue a warrant! Was it the blood? The police never mentioned it. Did they find it? Could they even process it that fast? What would they compare it to?

Sterling's tightly planned heist was being riddled with attacks from all sides. In addition, how perceptive was Detective Scott to see the possible link to Chapman. The problem with lying is in remembering the lie.

He had to go to work. His head was swimming. He had to focus; he had to work. Why won't they pick up the damn trash? Drip, a single drop of blood.

CHAPTER 8

―◆―▸―

VICTIM TURNED AGGRESSOR

"Good morning Boston. This is WGZ News. There was a murder/robbery at Forest Hills Jewelry store last night. Police said they had numerous leads and hope to have a suspect in custody soon. This makes the third murder in Bean Town this month alone."

"Now with traffic report is..."

Click.

Did Sterling hear correctly—MURDER/robbery? Who was murdered? Was it Chapman? No wonder the police were so vigilant. They are investigating a murder case not just a theft! They will use every resource at their disposal. His muscles tightened to the point he could hardly breath. He became very light headed as he stepped off the elevator at his office.

"Sterling, Mr. Fine would like to see you immediately in his office."

"Ok."

"Sterling; the police were here this morning with a search warrant and searched your office."

"You're being investigated in the Forest Hills Jewelry store robbery and murder. I know this is one of your accounts but why do they suspect you?"

"Mr. Fine, I don't know. All I can guess is because I worked in his office last week on his books," replied Sterling.

"Well, you know what this means," said Mr. Fine.

"I'm obviously off that account," said Sterling.

"Yes, and all other accounts until this mess is cleaned up. Cleaned up means the police have arrested and the courts convicted the murderer. Anything less leaves a doubt and we can't have any blemishes on our firm's good name."

"You're firing me?"

"No, you're resigning. Effective immediately and I'll accept your resignation."

"If I don't resign?"

"Then you'll be let go. I must caution you that by doing that you will also give up any reference of our firm, and that has a lot of value. Besides, once cleared, we might rehire you."

"You'll have my resignation today and thanks for your support (sarcastically spoken). And just for the record; I didn't murder anyone."

Sterling's world just kept deteriorating. First, he goes through a messy divorce; then his mother is murdered; the police suspect him of murder; he had the money to pay off Ned the Knee but can't access it, as he's being followed by the police; and now fired from his profession.

Enough! Enough! Thought Sterling. No more victim. Time to go on the offense. Let the chips fall where they may.

The best strategy in chess when losing is to attack the King. Take the opponent off guard. Use whatever assets you have left to attack.

First order of business; end the problem with Ned.

"Dad, I have what you need. You give Ned my cell phone number and have him call me 6 pm tonight. Understand?"

"Yes, but how—"

"No questions just do it. And Dad, you understand this is the one and only time I'm going to do this. Next time, Ned owns you. I will not help. Straighten out your act and do it now. You are the reason Mom's dead. We're done."

"I understand. But I do love you."

"Have him call me; 6 pm."

Ring.... Ring....

"Hello."

"Sterling, this is Manny. I wanted to remind you that you need to be packed and out of the apartment soon."

"No!"

"What do you mean no? It is in the court ruling."

"If you want me out; have me arrested. Otherwise I am staying. I'll leave when I'm ready."

"I'll do it Sterling."

"Fine – Do it."

Click.

Sterling kept stewing.

How was he going to get the money for Ned out of the locker? He was being watched 24 hours a day. He never figured on being tailed. Who was murdered anyway? Was it Chapman?

Then it hit him. Let Ned get it. The police are not following Ned. He could even send up one of his pawns to get the money. Even better, maybe Ned would take the black bag of Jewels instead. Sterling had no source to sell them. It was at least worth a try.

6:05 pm – Ring.... Ring....

"You're late. I said 6 pm to call me."

"Do you know who this is?"

"Yeah, I know who you are, and here's the deal. I have well over $40,000 in jewelry stored in a locker. Send up one of your pawns and I will give him the key and location. Even though the bag is sealed, send up someone you trust, so they do not take half for themselves."

"Then we're through. My father's debt is paid, and we never talk again."

"I don't want jewelry; I want cash," said Ned.

"Jewels, lots of jewels. Take it or leave it."

"I'll kill your father, slowly."

"Then do it." Click.

6:10 pm... Ring...Ring.

"Hello."

"Alright; Fine. But you understand this; if the value of the jewels is $1 less than $40,000; JR dies very, very slowly. Then I come after you."

"Better yet — I'll Fed Ex the key and location overnight; give me your PO Box. We're done."

Sterling felt pumped. This little pawn took on the Castle this time and won. He dictated the terms. He controlled the board, the game. It felt so good; just like winning at chess.

He sat down with his computer and started up a game online. He didn't even get a nose bleed.

CHAPTER 9

THE INVESTIGATION

Knock. Knock.

"Police – we need to talk to you Mr. Russell."

"What now?"

"Open the door, we have more questions. We can do it here or downtown, your choice."

"Fine but keep it short."

"Why? What's your hurry; you're not working now."

"Yeah, thanks to you. Because you have me as a suspect; I got fired."

"And in case you forget to ask me. No, I did not murder Chapman."

"Who said Chapman was murdered? Did you know Walter Broskavitch?"

"Who!"

"Walter Broskavitch."

"Never heard of him. Did he kill Chapman?"

"No one killed Chapman," said Detective Scott. "Why do you think he was killed?"

"I heard it on the radio; robbery and murder so I just thought it was Chapman."

"You've never heard of Broskavitch?"

"No, never."

"Not in any of Chapman's paperwork; on invoices?"

"No."

"Do you know where Chapman purchased his uncut diamonds?"

"No. He only purchased cut diamonds to my knowledge. Mostly from the brokerage – Diamond House I believe it was called."

"So, you claim to know nothing about illegal diamonds?"

"Correct."

"Do you know of any contacts with the Russian mob?"

"No."

"Let's go through where you were that night."

"We've been all through this already."

"Let us tell you what we have confirmed."

"At 7 pm, you spoke with to the landlord. He confirmed your story."

"At 7:30 you called one of your accounts; McKenzie Inc and at 7:45 a second call to Wards tools, both were confirmed by your phone records."

"At 9 pm your landlord fixed your toilet. We came here at 6:30 am. Where were you between 9 pm and 6:30 am?"

"In bed – Asleep."

"Can you prove that?"

"No."

"The murder took place early morning," said Detective O'Brien. "We know you're involved. The accountant always knows. Even if you didn't crush his skull; you know who did. You know the Russian connection; you know about the diamonds."

"You're holding out! Speak now and maybe we can cut you a deal. Wait and you can be charged with conspiracy, accomplice after the fact, impeding a police investigation amongst others. By the time you get out; the Dewey Decimal System will have been replaced."

"I can't help you; I don't know anything about a murder or diamonds."

"Ok. Have it your way – let's go!"

"Where?"

"To the station."

"Why?"

"Fingerprints, blood sample, hair sample and lots more questions."

"I won't give you any samples."

"Yes, you will, we have a warrant."

"And, may I remind you of your legal rights to a lawyer, before questions."

All Sterling could think of, was the blood. Where was the nose bleed? Did it happen in the jewelry store? Will they compare DNA? Did they find it?

"Yes; I have no money; no job now; I want a lawyer."

"Fine; let's go."

"Where?"

"To jail."

"Wait, why jail?"

"It's 7 pm; the court will appoint you a lawyer in the morning."

"No! No! No! I can't go to jail."

"Yes! Yes! Yes, you can. And, we can add resisting arrest if needed. Let's go."

"I promise you I won't go anywhere. Besides, you still have my car."

"Last time you convinced us because of your great job you won't run. What's to hold you now?"

"You have my word."

"Not good enough."

The police station was decrepit. Sterling was convinced it was built about 1900. The entire 1st floor used to be the horse stables and still had a wrenching odor of horse urine in the wooden floors, old steam pipes covered in gray ash; noisy metal stairs. The police station was every bit as horrible to Sterling as he had imagined.

The processing was just as unnerving. All items and his belt into a bag. Fingerprinted, blood; hair samples taken then brought downstairs to the holding cell.

His worst nightmare was happening. The cells were small, no, tiny. Each contained two bunk beds and a stainless-steel toilet with no seat and a small hand sink.

It was dark. The windows were few, small, barred and opaque. The floors were wet. A rat ran past his foot. The whole cell area smelled of urine, of vomit, of alcohol. It was dirty, oh so dirty.

"Come on – move it," said the officer with a nudge. Whether it was the nudge or if Sterling blacked out for a second; or if he just slipped on the slime on the floor, he fell.

"Disgusting." he murmured, as his hands slowly slid along the topping of the cement floor.

"Get in there," as they opened the cell and Sterling was looking at his roommates for the night.

The one on the left was a huge man, about 40; receding hair with a ponytail; two or three days of beard growth; arms the size of Sterling's leg with too many tattoos to count. He was filthy, smelled and had terrible breath! His only words were, "you go there," pointing to the top bunk on the other side.

Sterling was scared to death. He didn't say a word, only nodded and headed to other side. He touched the mattress and out skirted a half dozen cockroaches.

Then he met Bob. A small man in his 20's, clean cut.

"Hi, I'm Bob. I'm here for doing crack. Who are you?"

"Sterling; I'm charged with murder."

With that one word, the hierarchy of the cell changed. The two inmates were afraid of meek little Sterling. What a switch.

No one spoke the rest of the night. Sterling had no problem except he couldn't see peeing in the toilet with another's head only 12 inches away; so, he held it. He probably was not going to sleep anyway.

Breakfast was disgusting, powdered eggs of some sort and oatmeal. The place was dirty and must have broken every health code in the books. He could not wait to get back upstairs, even just to an interrogation room. That finally happened at 11 am.

"Sterling, this is your attorney, Ms. Sarah Murray. I'll leave you alone for thirty minutes."

Sterling didn't recognize Sarah, but she remembered him from setting up a blanket and umbrella most warm days on the beach for his mom at Ocean City. A high school summer crush doesn't fade very fast.

Sarah was a few years older than Sterling. She was tall and slender; and dressed like a top end lawyer. Sterling felt an immediate attraction toward Sarah. He saw hope in her eyes. Hope for freedom from this nightmare. Hope of a possible future and maybe even a future with her.

"I didn't kill anyone," offered Sterling.

"Good, keep that attitude," replied Sarah.

"No, I mean it. I really didn't kill anyone."

"Ok; but before you plead not guilty you should seriously consider the offer from the assistant DA.

They'll reduce the charge to Murder 2, 15 to life. With some luck and good behavior, you could be out in 15 years."

"If you plead not guilty and lose it's life without parole."

"But I'm innocent. I have done nothing wrong. I just spent the most miserable night of my life in jail. I do not want to ever spend another night in jail, ever. You must get me out today; now."

"Slow down Sterling," said Sarah.

"First things first. My specialty is drug cases. I have never defended a murder case. I will help you, but it will be between other cases as well. The DA's office has the state budget as its resource. Expert witnesses and forensics, manpower, a team of expert criminal lawyers. The state could probably get a conviction if you were out of state when this happened."

"Second, they have a very strong and believable case."

"Motive: You're broke, losing your apartment and car in a few weeks, a very expensive divorce settlement. Do you deny you need money?"

"No, but everyone needs money," replied Sterling.

"Sterling – In two weeks where are you sleeping? Where will you go?"

"I don't know!" shouted Sterling almost in tears. "I don't know. I don't know," he kept repeating.

"And didn't you feel angry at Chapman when he gave you so little for the diamond cross? He told the police you needed money. He showed a receipt for the $500 he paid you. He told police you wanted more and were upset."

Sterling was in shock. There was no receipt. It was $5500 not $500. What was Chapman trying to pull?

He never answered the lawyer.

"Now, let's talk opportunity."

"Were you in the Forest Hills backroom for about a week before the murder?"

"Yes. I was doing an internal audit."

"Chapman said you called him and said he was scheduled for a Federal audit. How would you know that?"

"That's not true. I told him that he COULD be audited. That's all."

"Your alibi until 9 pm is solid. In fact, very solid. But from 9 pm to 6:30 am you have no alibi. None. The murder happened early that morning. And then there's the forensics," said Sarah.

"As expected, your fingerprints are in the backroom. There was so much blood everywhere (showing photos). The police took dozens of samples and are processing DNA. Head wounds bleed a lot."

"He was shot in the head?" asked Sterling.

"No; there are numerous broken clocks in the back room. The police believe you contacted Broskavitch, broke into the store and he opened the safe. One of you decided to keep it all. You and Broskavitch struggled ending when you literally clocked him in the head."

"A death caused during the act of a felony is considered murder."

"They have a strong case, think about the plea bargain."

"No; no deals. I didn't kill Broskavitch; someone else did – how about Chapman? Let me guess, he found the body and called police."

"Correct."

"Sterling; hear me on this. This is a one-time offer by the DA's office. If you pass and they:

- Find a single drop of your blood anywhere
- Money or jewels from the store in your possession
- Your prints on the broken clocks
- Any forensics-prints, fibers, window glass on your clothes, on the safe

You'll spend the rest of your life in jail. Do you understand?"

"Yes."

"And you still want to plead not guilty."

"Yes."

"Ok. It's your life. Here's what happens next."

"I'll call the police in and advise you to answer absolutely none of their questions. Make them prove your guilt. Remember, they are out to hurt you, to send you to jail. It's personal. It has nothing to do with justice."

"Later today, we will go in front of a judge and enter your plea of not guilty. The DA will argue for no bail sighting high risk of flight. I will counter with your standing the community. Most likely the judge will set bail around $100-$300,000."

"Since your using a public defender I assume you can't raise bail, so you will be transferred to either Concord Prison or Billerica House of Correction until trial, probably for about 2 months or so."

"Two months," screamed Sterling. "In jail. No. I can't."

Drip.

"Sterling, you won't have a choice, I'll do what I can for you. But think about their offer."

The judge set bail at $250,000 cash no bond. Because of the lateness of the day, Sterling would be transferred in the morning, so he would spend another night down stairs. The second night in jail was even worse than his first. He considered suicide.

CHAPTER 10

THE RUSSIAN CONNECTION

At 9 am Sterling was in the process of being transferred when Detective O'Brien stepped in.

"Mr. Russell; bail has been posted. You are free to leave. By order of the court you cannot leave the Greater Boston area."

"Who posted the bail?"

"Like you don't know. Quit the act. Your friends in the Russian mob. The lawyer's name is a Mr. Pembroke, a known lawyer for Derek Sinski."

"Tell me again how you had no part in the murder?"

"I killed no one; you should be investigating Chapman."

"Your Russian friends are waiting."

Outside, the stretch limo looked like any other until they opened the door. It must have been almost a foot thick. The window glass alone was over an inch thick. Inside was a well-dressed man, three-piece suit;

starched, white shirt, conservative tie; gold cufflinks with large diamonds. He spoke with a slight Russian accent.

"Get in," spoken in a deep voice.

"Mr. Russell, we have some business to discuss. You have my jewels and I want them back."

"I don't know what you're talking about," said Sterling hoping his feelings of outright fear would not crack his voice.

"Mr. Russell, let's not, how you say, 'play games.' I know you broke into Chapman's safe and took what was mine. You have no way to sell them. Give them back to me. They are mine."

"If I did have them and gave you the black bag; you would kill me."

"And lose $250,000 bail money – not a chance. I want that back too. You will tell me. It can be as partner or through excruciating pain. But either way you WILL tell me."

"Hi, I'm Sterling Russell, your newest partner; and you are?"

"Just call me Derek. Now where is my bag?"

"The bag is gone. I owed $40,000 to Ned the Knee in Woodbridge, N.J. I gave him the bag of jewels from the safe to pay off the debt."

"$40,000."

"You gave him $240,000 worth of jewels. You are a fool. You are stupid."

"How do I find this Ned the Knee?"

"I have an address where I sent a lock box key. I should warn you; he is a bad person; murdered my mother. Do not underestimate him," as Sterling removed a small piece of paper from his wallet that contained the P.O. Box number and handed it to Derek.

"Do not worry yourself about Ned the Knee. Your debt to him is over. You will never hear from me again or Ned for that matter. That is unless you are lying to me. Are you lying to me?"

"No."

"Good, you do not ever want to lie to me. Or; if you do not show up for trial, I'll be watching; do not skip bail. I will find you."

"I'll be at the trial because I did not kill Broskavitch. I may have stolen from the safe but that's all I did."

"Broskavitch was a loyal trusted member of my family," said Derek. "His death will not go unavenged. But I believe in handling business before pleasure."

"Good day Mr. Russell and keep your mouth shut or I do have a solution if it opens. You understand?"

As Sterling exited the limo, he saw two plain clothes police officers taking photos. That will go over big at the trial, he thought. Just then, the sun broke through a cloud and shined brightly on Sterling's face. It felt so warm, so good. Feelings of calm; of a time long ago with his mom at the beach, when life was simpler. It felt wonderful. Sterling smiled.

Click, went the police officer's camera. Reality rushed back in.

Drip.

Sterling spent most of the remaining day drinking alone at the bar that is until he was escorted briskly out of the bar with a person under each of his arms. If he wasn't so drunk, he would have been petrified; instead he only saw his father's image. That was not an image he liked. It created a deep gut reaction of what he had become.

CHAPTER 11

THE SAFE HOUSE

"Who are you two? Why do you want me? Where are you taking me and Why?" slurred Sterling.

"I am Special Agent Nett of the Boston F.B.I.'s organized crime unit. This is Special Agent Bronick."

"What could you possibly want with me?" Sterling asked.

"First we need to know what just transpired in the limo. What did you and Sinski talk about?" asked Special Agent Nett.

"Who is Sinski?" a troubled and drunk Sterling asked.

"Derek Sinski, commander of the Russian Mob in Boston," answered Bronick.

"Oh, you mean my new partner, Derek. SHURRRRRR, it's a secret," whispered Sterling.

Although Sterling was confused and dazed, he refused to tell them. He kept remembering Derek's implied threats to keep quiet or he would have Sterling killed. The alcohol was starting to really kick in.

"I know my rights. You cannot question me without my law person with me. You would like her, she's hot. Her name is Mary, or Murray or; Oh, Oh, I know, Sarah something. Get Sarah."

"Sterling, we do not need Sarah. In fact, it will be safer for Sarah if she is not involved." responded S.A. Nett. "We know you are an upright citizen that wants to help your country and fellow citizens. Your country is asking for your help in putting a Russian mob boss out of business in Boston. Will you help us, and tell us about the limo?"

"No, get Sarah."

"We know you even helped save the President's life at Bentley. I know you want to do the right thing. Tell us what happened." added S.A. Nett.

"NEED SARAH," Sterling shouted as his nose started to drip blood.

"Enough, start talking now," growled S.A. Bronick.

"GET SARAH," Sterling screamed as he passed out.

The road was obviously dirt. Sterling could hear the pebbles bouncing off the inner fender walls. The air smelled of fresh manure. He could not tell if it was day or night because of the black hood covering his entire head. Sterling felt the cold steel of the handcuffs pressing against the car floor.

As he awoke, he was still confused and quite inebriated. He groveled, "Take off the hood, please take off the hood."

"Hey Don, (S.A. Nett), our guest has awoken," came from Bronick.

"We will be at the safe house, it is only a few more miles. It is for all of our protection no one knows where the safe house is located." Nett answered Sterling.

"Where is Sarah?" asked Sterling.

"We do not need Sarah. In fact, as I said before, it will be safer for Sarah," answered S.A. Nett.

The car pulled up to a large old house, part of a former working farm. The fields were still being used by commercial farmers renting space, growing mostly corn. The outside the house needed much repair. Shutters were falling off. The paint was chipped. Bushes and lawns were overgrown. The house looked much run down and in disrepair.

The barns and attached silo were in worse condition. Vines grew heavy on the partially collapsed barn and all the way to the top of the silo. Old rusted farm equipment littered the fields. The fields were very long but relatively shallow, with the tree line at most 200 yards away.

The house appeared to be constructed around the turn of the 20th century. Three sides were covered with the large farmer's porch. The house faced south, and you could see the stumps of the two shade trees used in that era to cool the house in summer, then drop leaves to keep it sunny in the winter. Out back was the large screened in summer kitchen including three rusted wood burning stoves used for canning the farm products.

Entering the first room on the right was like passing through a portal into a future time zone. The doors were large and made of stainless steel. The room was a completely self-contained enclosure; like a panic room.

Four sets of bunks lined the left wall, to the right a large pantry of food and other supplies. Also, there was a partitioned toilet and shower. The right wall (backing up to the front of the house) was full of computers, video monitors showing both the outside of the farm and the inside of the house. A locked weapons rack contained M16 rifles, shotguns, a sniper rifle, and even four rocket launchers.

Bragging about the room, the agent monitoring the screens added, "We also have both conventional and radio communication abilities. The room has a fire suppression system and a remote generator for power if outside service is cut."

"We have our own air intake and enough oxygen to survive three hours. Under that rug is a sealed culvert that as a last case option brings us underground to the tree line. We have rescue troops at Concord, twenty minutes away, and local police, state patrol, and fire departments even closer. You are safe here," the agent assured Sterling.

All this security made Sterling feel more and more nervous. Why is he in this secure of a place? Also, in thinking about chess, there are very few defenses that cannot be overcome with planning and the right tools.

Sterling broke into an alarmed jewelry store, then it's safe, with no prior experience, just good planning.

As Sterling was thinking how he would overcome these defenses, S.A. Nett started up again; "You should feel safe now, so it is time for you to tell us about that meeting with Sinski in the limo."

"No, bring Sarah here first."

For the rest of the day the two Special Agents took turns trying to get Sterling to talk. They tried promises, coercion, even physical threats, but all to no avail. Sterling kept remembering Sinski's threat to 'deal with him' if he talked. Especially after hearing about all the 'safety features' in the safe house, Sterling's money was on Sinski. Every advantage could be overcome. Why would they even brag about the features to a person that did not need to know? The best security starts with it being a secret.

Sterling could visualize an attack that started with cutting the wires on the only poles that ran beside the dirt road. Down goes conventional communications, and power. With a portable jammer disable the radio communications. Without power the video cameras, computers, and monitors, all switch to a battery backup while the generator starts up and comes online. Listen carefully, generators are noisy. Find the generator and disable it quietly by blocking the air intake, or if needed using explosives.

Fire suppression is great for putting out a fire but would be useless if the house was engulfed in flames.

The goal is to kill the people in the safe room; a large fire would work well.

Separate air intake for the room, find it and contaminate it. Even a small amount of tear gas would be enough. Separate oxygen supply....the fire idea is getting stronger.

The culvert escape tube is a good idea but that can also work in the attackers' favor. The tube is also a way of going from the tree line unseen directly to the floor of the safe room. Drill a hole and add gas, blow the hatch; those possibilities are endless. Sterling kept thinking he would keep the attack simple, probably fire.

By early afternoon the two agents gave up and went to pick up Sarah. Four hours later a hooded and furious Sarah arrived.

Sarah did not say a word while the two agents presented their case for needing Sterling to testify.

Finally speaking for the first time. "So, what is in it for Sterling? Obviously, all charges would be dropped and at least three years of witness relocation and protection; for a start."

"We can drop all federal charges and obtain witness protection services, provided what he has to say is of value, and he agrees to testify in federal court." answered Nett.

"It must include all state charges being dropped as well." Sarah added.

"I cannot promise that. The state has a very strong case of murder and I do not think they will agree to drop the case," said S.A. Nett.

"How inept of a lawyer do you think I am?" Sarah was getting more and more angry. "Do you really think I would advise my client to take a deal that could end with his witness protection starting immediately after he completes his life sentence for murder? You want Sterling to talk you need to bargain with the state D.A. first and it better be a show stopper of a deal."

S.A. Nett agreed to meet with the D.A. first thing in the morning. S.A. Nett and S.A. Bronick headed to Boston to prepare their arguments. Sarah was escorted to the safe room where Sterling was happily surprised.

"Sarah, I am so glad to see you, let me tell you what has been happening." Sterling said excitingly.

Sarah put one finger to his lips and said, "Quiet. Everything we say is being recorded. Only say things you would say if S.A. Nett was in the discussion also. Say nothing about some limo the two agents were discussing, some person named Derek Sinski, and especially the court case. Even if you whisper, it will be recorded."

Sterling could tell by Sarah's expressions and tone, she was very upset, and angry with him; and this entire situation. Sterling was attracted to Sarah, and it was important that he had her friendship as much as her legal skills. "I am truly sorry you are now in danger and in the middle of this mess," holding both of Sarah's hands. "Please forgive me."

Speaking softly, Sterling cautioned Sarah, "Do not trust the security of this room. If Sinski wants us it would not be hard for these security measures to be overcome, especially with any tie to former K.G.B. personnel or equipment. I just saw Nett and Bronick leave meaning there are only two agents guarding the fort, the one on the monitors and one outside at the road. We also do not know where their loyalty lies. Do they have a second income?"

"K.G.B.? How much trouble are we in?" a now more concerned than angry Sarah asked.

Sterling's apology went a long way toward mending their relationship.

Also, Sarah could see that Sterling was equally the victim in this situation and knew it would take teamwork to survive if the safe house were to be attacked.

"If something does happen, that floor hatch is probably our best escape. While we wait, let's watch the monitors; six eyes are better than two." As Sterling pointed toward the screens.

CHAPTER 12

THE ATTACK

"STOP! You are on the wrong road", yelled the agent outside. An eighteen-wheel water truck, (like the ones used in the neighboring corn fields), came to a quick stop. "Back it up," he added.

"It is over a mile back before I could turn this beast, let me spin it around just ahead and drive out?" asked the driver.

Before the agent could refuse, a muffled thud of a sniper rifle's bullet was heard, and the agent fell instantly to the ground.

The truck rolled forward, then swung around to make a straight line back to the farm house. A super charged diesel pushing 60,000 pounds of water at twenty miles an hour is almost unstoppable. It would easily take a house off its fieldstone foundation and destroy any added reinforcements. Also, even if the first hit punched a hole in the water tank, the driver could easily ram the house repeatedly.

However, it only took one hit. The massive truck crushed the foundation, walls, and poured water into the room. The rear truck wheels pushed past the foundation walls and dropped into the cellar cavity not allowing any more rams.

Inside the room the agent was pinned under the wall. He handed Sterling his hand gun. In seeing no hope for the pinned agent, he handed it back and told him to, "keep count of the rounds, save at least one for yourself if needed."

The agent told them, "to go out the trap door, but listen carefully. Make sure you relock the hatch from inside so no one can follow you. There are flashlights at the base of the tube. Follow the tube until it ends in the tree line. At the exit hatch you will find hiker packs with money, clothes, supplies, and maps to help with your escape. They will expect you to go south so head north. GO! GO! Fast! They are coming. I will buy you as much time as I can."

The powerful hit from the water truck lifted the room, escape tube and all, about 12 inches up. The door latch somehow still worked.

Sarah dropped in first, then Sterling. He locked the hatch as Sarah turned on the flashlights. The culvert was broken where the truck moved the floor. You could peek out and see the truck wheels of the tanker.

Like two moles, Sarah and Sterling on hands and knees traversed the pipe. Mud in the bottom of the pipe soothed Sarah's knees. Although it felt like hours, they reached the exit hatch in less than fifteen minutes. Before opening the door, they inventoried the hiker packs, both were the same.

A small caliber handgun and 5-inch folding knife
Crank radio and flashlight
Night vision goggles
First aid kit
Matches and survival guide
Maps and compass
Signal mirror and whistle
Hiker's sneakers and stretch clothes including a poncho
Sleeping roll
Hair dye, scissors, and camouflage paint sticks
Two waters and various food bars
Five thousand dollars cash.

Given it was almost dusk, they decided to wait until dark in the tunnel. It also gave them time to look over the maps, and to change into the hiker's clothes. They were not excited about wearing the night vision goggles but knew it would give them an advantage by staying inside the tree lines for cover and help also where the terrain in much rougher. As they left the tube, they could clearly see the farm house completely engulfed in flames.

As they walked, Sterling started to recognize different features of the surroundings. He remembered the right angle turn of the dirt road where it adds a full lane. On the corner is a sugar shack with wood stock piled for the spring boil down. He has been here before as a child. The memories came flooding back of the

November hunting trips with his father in the Parker Mountain Range. He turned to Sarah and said, "Put away the goggles. We are on 'Cannan Back Road', near the Strafford New Hampshire town line. The Isinglass Inn on Bow Lake is less than two miles ahead. We can stay on the road as two hikers heading for the inn. The inn would be the perfect place to hide and for us to make plans of what to do next. Before we go on, tuck all your hair under the cap so no one will see the real color before it is dyed."

"Given the intensity of the fire it will be a long time before the F.B.I. know if we died in the fire, or were taken by Sinski's men, or just ran off. The local fire, then state inspectors will take time to investigate. Eventually, the F.B.I. will figure we used the tube because of it being locked from the inside. I would also guess that the Russian's would have looked in and seen that we were not in the room before they set the fire."

CHAPTER 13

OFF THE GRID

It was now evening, and Sterling and Sarah were at the dam where Bow Lake empties into the start of the Isinglass River. They stopped at the corner store appropriately named the Dam Stop. As promised, across the street was the old Isinglass Inn, a perfect place to stay. No computers, no WIFI, poor or no cell phone service, lucky if T.V. even came in.

"Hey, the no vacancy light isn't on."

"Good evening folks and welcome to the Isinglass Inn. You're lucky; we had a last-minute cancellation, so I have a room available, must be fate; up until 15 minutes ago we were full."

"We'll take it," said Sarah. "Here let me sign the registry." Mr. and Mrs. Marsella

The owner never asked about luggage.

Drip! "Sorry," as Sterling wipes the blood off the Inn's registry counter.

The room was quaint, early New England. It was cooled by a ceiling fan. The old cast iron radiator stood proudly as a monument of a different time. The bed was comfy looking with a red and brown patchwork quilt, and two overstuffed pillows. There was a mixture of gourds and potpourri on the old dresser. There was no bathroom in the room; it was at the end of the hall, only a small wash basin in the room.

As Sterling entered the room, he felt confused, rushed with conflicting feelings. Happy to be there with Sarah, hopeful of spending the night together, nervous, that he might do something wrong; guilty of the pretense; it felt like his very first date, or very first kiss. He also had no idea of what Sarah expected or didn't expect. What if he went too far? What if he doesn't go far enough?

However, of all the mixed feelings, happy was by far in the lead.

They spent the next hour helping each other change appearances. Sterling cut off much of Sarah's long hair and helped her dye it a darker shade of brown. Sterling liked the look, "it makes you even more adorable."

Sarah suggested shaving Sterling's head bald, but Sterling felt it would be to obvious, better to just lighten his hair. They both should wear hats if outside to hide their hair and face.

Sterling suggested they visit the dining room soon before the kitchen closes.

"The roast beef is incredible, cooked perfectly," noted Sarah. "Can we get a second glass of wine?"

After dinner, they spent an hour in front of the lobby fireplace, sipping wine but trying not to talk, only listen.

Over the fireplace was a large empty wooden oval; underneath was a nameplate, "Bert". Sterling asked the innkeeper John, "why the plaque?"

In his best put-on New Hampshire accent, John the owner responded, "Holding that spot for the legendary Bert the Bass."

"Who?" asked Sterling?

"Bert."

"You name your fish here," asked Sarah.

"Ah-yup; we did this one," answered John.

Sarah leans over and whispers, "I hope I didn't just eat Betsy the cow for supper." and giggles. Sarah pours herself another glass of wine.

"Can you tell us why Bert's a legend?" asked Sterling.

"Sure can," he replied continuing his New Hampshire accent, as he sat on an overstuffed chair.

"There's many legends and fish stories about Bow Lake; but Bert the bass is the most known. So, the story goes, twenty years ago; a new camp owner off Brown's Pasture Road went a fishin' with his four young'uns. They anchored in a small cove across from Bennett Island."

"Using a popper, he made his first cast and Wham! A bass grabbed that hook and jumped two feet out the water. After a long contest, the fish was brought on board and placed in the side-holding tank, in the front of the boat."

"That bass was lunch. He could taste that bass painted with butter on the grill. As the legend goes; now all excited his second cast sent that popper 30 feet up a tree on shore. And that tree kept that popper. He fished for another hour but not even as much as a nibble."

"During that hour his four young'uns were fascinated with that fish. They looked at him and tried to pet him. By the time they got home, that fish had changed from lunch, to Bert the Bass, a pet. They let him go in their beach area. He stayed for a long time under a paddleboat; then was gone."

"Since then, Bert has been hooked many a times but NEVER landed. We get stories in here from fishermen all the time about poles pulled overboard; broken lines; got him out of the water but he jumped off. We tell them –yup– probably Bert."

"Well folks, I'm turning in," said the owner. "Please turn off the lights when you go upstairs."

"Oh; we'll turn in now also," said Sarah. As she stood up, she almost tipped over. "Wow; you serve strong wine."

Sterling helped her upstairs. As he opened the door, she fell on the bed. "Whew! I'm lit."

"How do we do this? What's the arrangement?" asked Sterling.

"Well; there's only one bed and no chair, so we can share the bed but no funny business. We'll sleep in our skivvies."

"Ok," agreed Sterling. He felt honored just to share the bed and lie that close.

Sarah started to unbutton her blouse as she lay on the bed. She told Sterling, "Close your eyes."

After much difficulty, she removed her blouse and pants and snuck into bed.

Sterling covered his eyes with his hands the entire time. He also peeked.

"Your turn," said Sarah.

Sterling fumbled with his shirt and belt buckle. Almost embarrassed, he slipped into the left side of the bed.

"Ok, you can uncover your eyes," said Sterling. She peeked too.

They both felt very strange, each lying on their backs looking up at the ceiling, each not knowing what to do.

Sarah slowly grabbed Sterling's left hand with her right. They both blushed. It must have been the wine. Sarah turned on her right-side facing Sterling, still clutching his left hand and placed her left hand on his stomach. Her thumb fell into his belly button.

He instantly jumped and put his hand on top of hers not knowing what to expect next.

Finally, she whispered in his ear, "sweet dreams and thank you for the supper. See you in the morning."

She gave him a nibble on his ear and rolled over to sleep.

Sterling lay content on his side for twenty minutes then turned over and just watched Sarah sleep.

Like the bass stories from Bow Lake, Sterling was hooked!

CHAPTER 14

THE LAKE

Just outside the Inn is the dam area, consisting of a Grange hall, public dock, public beaches on both sides of the dam spill way, and the Dam Stop country store. The far side of the beach was mostly shady with benches. The close side was all sun. Both swim areas were sandy and refreshingly cool.

Sterling could see that John the Innkeeper needed money and Sterling needed a car. However, with no ID or license they had no way of renting or even buying a car because of no way to register it.

"Want a quick hundred dollars? Just let me borrow your car for a run up to Rochester, and no questions asked." Sterling asked John.

"Yes," answered John, "provided you fill the gas tank first and Sarah stays in the Inn until I get my car keys back."

Sterling and Sarah had already made up a list of items.

Swimwear for both including towels, hats, trunks, and a wrap for Sarah.

More serious survival gear.

Writing paper, pens, envelopes, and stamps.

Sterling was careful to keep under the speed limits and he drove straight to the center of town passing many of the large chain stores. The stores in the center of town were much more expensive with less selection, but they also have no cameras for facial recognition. The only store not in the center was an Army Navy store he passed on the way. There he picked up sleeping bags, mess kits and similar army surplus of the 70's.

Because it was July 4th, the entire beach area was packed with people celebrating. The air was full of great BBQ aromas, and happy sounds of children laughing and splashing in the water. When Sterling returned to the Inn, Sarah was anxious to join the life at the beach and to leave the heat of the old inn. After changing into her bathing suit, she covered herself with the wrap and broad, brimmed hat, then asked Sterling, "Did you pick out this suit?"

Hesitating, "Kinda," he answered. "The shop owner's 14-year-old daughter picked it out for me. I figured she would have better taste than me. I told her to pick out something she would like in a size four."

Sarah stood in front of Sterling and undid the wrapping, "you 'kinda 'picked this out?"

In Sterling's eyes, Sarah was stunning. She looked even taller with her short hair and natural long neck.

The top was fine, but the string bikini bottom was so small Sarah even commented, "I have seen more cotton in a bottle of aspirin. Sterling. See that little store over there? They sell shorts, size four. GO! GO NOW! RIGHT NOW! SHORTS, SIZE 4! NOW!"

Sterling's nose started to drip. Sterling was back within minutes and they both went to the shady side of the beach and cooled off in the water.

However, even with shorts, hat and wrap, Sarah's natural beauty kept drawing attention. Stranger after stranger would hit on her asking questions, "Where are you from? Are you staying on the lake? How long are you staying? Do you have a boyfriend?"

It was obvious they needed a new place to hide.

The one-day distraction was needed and welcomed by both Sarah and Sterling, but it was time to address their situation.

Sterling took a chance and confided in John. He asked for his confidence and, "help in finding them a safe place to hide, also where they could get a car."

"Off Province road there are abandoned scout cabins that old man Greg Locke rents from time to time, mostly in the fall to hunters. They are nothing fancy but would keep you warm, dry, and bug free for the summer. The cabins have a small kitchen, large porch, and access to outhouses and the lake for bathing or swimming. I will see Greg tomorrow at the Grange meeting. If you offered him say $100 a week, I think he would bite." responded John.

"Will he want reference checks, ask many questions," John interrupting said, "No. Not Greg Locke. If he does not like you, he will just run you off with his 12 gauge."

"The car is another matter. As I see it you have two choices," said John. "First use my old Jeep. The sticker is valid until September and the plates are good even longer. You pay me $3000 and I will buy another car, and have it registered and insured. At the end of summer, I keep both cars. It may sound like a lot, but I do need a car to run the Inn."

"Your second option I could connect you with Dave, a fella that picks up old and dead cars for their scrap value. He could find you one that still runs and has a valid inspection sticker. You would have to steal a license plate off someone else's car. I also cannot guarantee that Dave would not turn you in himself, so he could repossess the car and sell it again."

"We will take the Jeep." answered Sterling.

Sarah was watching 6, the only T.V. channel with a picture, (even if it was mostly snow), out of Portsmouth N.H. There was still no mention of the farm or the fire. Total blackout!

After the Grange meeting John told Sterling, "All set with the cabin. Pick out any one you want, none are locked." John also asked, "a number of the volunteer firefighters were at the meeting and were talking about the old James farm house was burnt to the ground. The locals called in the state police.

Something must be up because it was sealed off like a crime scene while they investigate."

"Happened the same day you folks showed up here. You folks have anything to do with the fire?"

"Nope. Why, did we smell like smoke?"

"No. No. You did not." John answered.

"We are just hiding from my wife, and her two crazy brothers," Sterling added.

Sterling went to his room and came back with $3400 that he gave to John for the car and cabin.

Two days later they drove to the old scout camp to pick out a cabin. Each was a carbon copy of the others. They looked first at one by the beach area, but it was in direct sun light with no shade. The next closest to the water was leaning and had water damage on the top mattress. They settled on a cabin under the pines and near the outhouse. It was a short walk to the beach area and inside was in decent shape. All the cabins had a rich musty smell that reminded Sterling of tenting with his father on the hunting trips.

The cabin had four sets of bunk bed frames like the ones used in the WWII barracks. The bunks were a simple frame with a wire mesh supported by three-inch springs. Unroll a two-inch mattress and the bunks are incredibly comfortable. The sleeping bags Sterling purchased at the Army Navy store fit perfectly although they did carry an odor. The table was made of slabs of pine thick cut and covered with a heavy coat of polyurethane. The sink had no running water but there was a hand pump in the common area. The sink drain emptied outside just into stone. The cabins were wired but all power had been turned off to the area. Two kerosene hurricane lamps still worked fine and added a simple charm to the nights. The cabins were cool day and night and the screened in porch had rockers that Sarah and Sterling both enjoyed.

Each morning Sterling would drive to the Dam Stop and pick up the, *Union Leader* and *Boston Globe* along with two coffees. They would read both papers cover to cover looking for any news related to Sinski or the farm house and fire. Nothing was in any of the papers.

After breakfast they would go to the lake to bath, swim, and sunbathe. The area was so desolate; Sarah would sometimes even let Sterling enjoy her suit without the added shorts.

Sarah heard a car on the gravel road and instantly put on her shorts. Around the corner came a Police car. Sterling joined Sarah and together they approached the vehicle.

Out of the police car stood a six-and-a-half-foot giant. "Morning folks, where you from?"

"Massachusetts," answered Sterling as his nose started to drip blood slowly.

"What brings you to our town?" he followed up.

"I have always loved the lake. As a child I would come here with my dad. Greg Locke gave us a good deal on renting a cabin for July, so we grabbed it," responded Sterling.

"Well, Welcome. Oh, and just a reminder, no open fires allowed except in the metal stands; we cannot afford a forest fire," as the officer opened his door.

"No problem officer, we will only use the stands," as instructed.

Sarah brought back reality, "Sterling, as fun as this has been, we need to discuss our next steps."

"You mean the murder charges?" asked Sterling.

"Those also, but we have a more immediate problem named Sinski that wants you or us dead. We cannot trust the F.B.I. as proven by the farm house. It was only a day from our arrival until the attack. Someone on the inside had to tell Sinski. That informant is still active. If we go to the FBI agents our bodies would not be found until hunting season," Sarah added sternly.

"We should follow our first plan. I can give the F.B.I. what they wanted in a letter describing the conversation in that limo. We can keep our location secret by using the letter in a letter plan we previously discussed. I will draft the inside letter addressed to the F.B.I. Major Crimes in Washington, D.C." suggested Sterling.

"I will close giving them instructions on how to communicate with me via the *BOSTON GLOBE* using the personals."

"Sarah, you draft the cover letter for inside the larger envelopes."

Sarah addressed four large envelopes, one each to a small town in Kentucky, New York, Ohio, and

California. Each was addressed to an unreadable written name at 223 Main Street.

They would drive to Brattleboro, VT. And drop the four letters into a street mailbox. At least one of the four should make it back to the F.B.I.

As they sat in the car for the ride to Vermont, Sarah said, "Stop the car. We need a better idea. If this plan works, no one can find us until we show up at a court house. We know there is an informant so how can we trust either when or where to show up. We also have no deal with the state D.A.'s office. If they get your letter, they no longer need to deal meaning no witness protection. You have never told me what you and Sinski discussed in the limo. But guessing, I'd say you would probably need federal protection after the trial."

"You are right." Sterling added, "What we really need is a person we can trust. Sarah, do you have anyone from the court systems that you would trust with our lives?"

"Sorry, no. No one"

"Do you Sterling?" she asked.

"Actually, I might, but it will be a challenge to reach him. Remember, I told you I helped save the President of the United States my senior year at Bentley?"

"Yes, I do."

"He might help us, but I doubt it because it would expose him to a charged murderer. Imagine the headlines, 'President helps murder suspect with

Russian mob connections avoid the F.B.I.' Never happen!"

"However, during the incident, I met an Agent Lavery of the Secret Service. The President knew him as he used to protect the First Daughter. I believe he is a man we could trust, but how do we get to him?"

CHAPTER 15

TO WASHINGTON

That evening in the cabin, Sterling was making notes about how he could ask for Secret Service Agent Lavery's help. At the same time Sarah was reading the papers as they did daily but still no mention of the safe house or the investigation, even after ten days.

In roared two pickup trucks of teenagers with radios blaring, complete with beer coolers, firewood, food and chairs. Apparently, this was a party spot for the locals. Sterling and Sarah stayed in the cabin and quickly turned off the lantern, so they would not be seen.

As the evening progressed, so did the party. It grew louder with a much brighter fire. Some were dancing, some went swimming in the lake, a few were fighting; just teenagers raising cane. Two more truck loads then arrived.

"You remember Andre the Giant in the police car? We should be seeing him soon," commented Sarah.

As she was making the comment a black shadow walked past the cottage toward the party. He stopped and rose up a shotgun and released one chamber.

"BOOM!"

Sparks and embers flew out of the barrel. The explosion echoed off the hills five or six times before fading. In his equally deep booming voice Greg Locke announced, "Party's over. You, Nelson, put out that fire. Leave the coolers. Do it now. I will not say it again."

Within a minute, the group had vanished, and Greg walked back to his farm.

"Sarah, we just saw one man by himself send twenty-five or more running because he was there. That is how we get a hold of Agent Lavery; we go see him in person in Washington D.C."

"Yes, Greg Locke was one man, but he did have a shotgun. And if I may cross examine;"

"How many years since you spoke with S.S. Agent Lavery?"

"Is Lavery still an agent?"

"Why do you think the Secret Service is called the SECRET service?"

"The agency would want to keep agent's identity a secret so that they, their family, or loved ones are not threatened. That type of blackmail is extremely powerful. All I am saying is it will not be as easy as walking to the gate and asking to see S.S.A. Lavery." added Sarah.

"So, I go to the guard shack by myself," proposed Sarah. "I ask to see Agent Lavery in whatever secure room they have. Even if Lavery is not still working, or available; as long as it is the Secret Service and not the F.B.I. we will be OK. I will ask them for help."

"First, they must agree not to notify the F.B.I. at least not yet."

"Second, research what happened at the safe house and Sinski."

"Third, how we can find someone to trust."

"If they refuse, I will threaten to bring up with the press how an accused murderer with connections to the Russian Mob saved the President's life."

"Whether I meet with S.S.A. Lavery or some other S.S. Agent, I think we need to trust that person."

Sterling agreed.

"Do not be surprised if they hold me for a few days while they sort this out and confirm my statements."

The road trip to Washington was long, slow and hot. They kept to only back roads to avoid toll cameras. For the same reason they kept the top of the Jeep covered. They stayed one night at a campground using the old army tent and sleeping bags. Although it kept them warm, it left a distinct unpleasant odor. Sarah bathed in the stream using just a washcloth and bar of soap before taking a taxi to the White House gate. Sterling washed her back.

Drip.

"Good morning, do you have a pass or invitation?" asked the White House guard.

"No sir. I came to see Secret Service Agent Lavery."

"Sorry", the guard responded. "There is no one here by that name. My I ask the nature of your business?"

Sarah answered, "Yes, but it is rather lengthy and complicated. I would appreciate meeting with either Agent Lavery or someone else in the Secret Service to explain."

"You read my mind Madame. Secret Service Agent Todd will escort you to just such a place where you can detail your reason for coming here today," said the guard.

In a closed room with an obvious one-way glass mirror, Sarah waited. After what seemed like hours, the door finally opened as two agents entered.

"Hello, I am Agent Wolf and you already met Agent Todd. May we see your ID?"

"Before I give you my name, I need to know if either of you or anyone behind that glass has any direct ties to the F.B.I. My life depends on the truth, and on the F.B.I. not knowing I am here, at least not yet."

"We are Secret Service agents and have no direct connections to the F.B.I. With that said, we are federal agents and work with the F.B.I. on domestic intelligence, just like we work with the C.I.A. on international issues, Homeland Security, the N.S.A. and a host of others. Now what is this all about?"

"My name is Sarah Murray. I am a lawyer in Massachusetts and represent Sterling Charles Russell in a robbery and murder charge of the Forest Hills Jewelry Store a little over a month ago. The F.B.I. took my pocket book and ID when they kidnapped separately both Sterling then myself and drove us to a 'safe house' to extract testimony against a key Russian Mob leader named Sinski."

"We were put into a 'Panic Room' in an old farmhouse. The farm was attacked, one day after our arrival. Someone in the F.B.I. Boston Organized Crimes unit must have informed Sinski for it to happen that fast."

"After killing the guard on the road, they backed a large truck into the farmhouse crushing the house and room. Then they set it on fire and it burned to the ground. The two Agents at the farm were both killed. Two other Agents, (Nett, and Bronick), were at the state D.A.'s office trying to work a deal for Sterling's testimony or at least that is what we were told by them. Seems lucky for them they were not at the farm. We escaped out a pipe in the room designed for that purpose and have been in hiding ever since."

"The point of me being here is to simply find someone we can trust, so we are gambling our lives on the honor of the Secret Service, especially Agent Lavery. Ask Agent Lavery about how my client, Sterling, helped save the President's life 2 years ago. Agent Lavery was there. He can testify about Sterling's roll. Will you help us?"

"First we need to check out your story," said Agent Todd.

"Please, it is not a 'story'. It is what happened," answered Sarah the lawyer.

"Sarah, we need to first confirm your identity. It would also help if Sterling came in as well."

"Not a chance," said Sarah. "Sterling dropped me off at the taxi stand and I told him not to tell me what state he was going to next. Also, whatever method you use to verify my identity, be it fingerprints, DNA, facial recognition or something else, just make sure it will not send a red flag to the F.B.I."

Agent Todd responded, "We have you covered and have been working on your Identity behind the mirror since you came into the room."

"Sarah, what was the name of the second-grade student that you pushed the ice-cream cone into his face?"

"Josh?" making a very surprised face.

"And what was 'Blue' at your mother's recent wedding?"

"She wore a blue sapphire ring on the back of her gown, her mother's."

"Would you like to say 'Hi' to your mom? She is on video camera on the computer behind you."

"MOM." Sarah called out.

"Sarah, I have been so worried about you. You always call but not a word in over two weeks. And what did you do to your hair?"

"Mom, I just trimmed it a little shorter, and darkened it some."

"Well I think it is adorable."

Agent Todd interrupting, "Sorry to cut this short, but for the record and under oath, you are stating to us that this is your daughter?"

"Absolutely."

As she predicted, Sarah stayed as a guest of the Secret Service for two days while they traced information; checked and rechecked each detail. Finally, a meeting was called to discuss what they found out.

Entering the room was Agent Todd, Agent Wolf, Agent Lavery, and the Director of the Secret Service himself at the President's request. They all stood at attention until the Director asked them to be seated.

Agent Lavery spoke, "most of what you told us was accurate with just a few exceptions."

"Yes. The Boston F.B.I. Major Crimes Unit did abduct you both for your protection and as a possible material witness against Sinski."

"Yes. The safe house was compromised, and two agents were killed."

"Yes. No one knows where you and Sterling have been hiding."

"But, the F.B.I. was on a fishing expedition. They had no idea of the content of the limo conversations. Most importantly, Sinski was sending a message to the F.B.I. Major Crimes Unit. Their target was the safe house and the agents; not you. Sinski's message was simply that no place is safe or out of his reach. Sinski probably did not even know you were in the safe room."

"How would you know any of this?" asked Sarah.

"We have our sources, but, are not at liberty to discuss them." answered S.S.A. Lavery. "Trust me, you are not in danger as long as Sterling shows up for the trial. That trial date is in five days, we wish you well," closed Agent Lavery.

CHAPTER 16

————— ◆► —————

JUDGE CULLUM

"Thank you, Your Honor, for allowing this meeting on the Defense request for a sixty-day postponement of the trial," opened Sarah. "Both my client and I were almost killed in a vicious attack that killed two F.B.I. Agents. We have both been in hiding since for fear of our lives. Being incommunicado kept us alive but, gave us no time to prepare for Sterling's Defense." added Sarah.

"Sterling, not Mr. Russell," interrupted the D.A. "And, if you two have been hiding out together, I believe you had plenty of time to strategize a defense. No interruptions," added the D.A. with a smirk.

Sarah jumped in, "First I object to the inuendo. Yes, we did talk some about the case. But, when you think your life is in danger, priorities change rapidly. We were focused on staying alive, not the trial. Second, there could be no depositions issued to question witnesses, no office services, no Discovery, no access to expert witnesses, no way to review the D.A.'s witness list never mind any forensics. Your Honor, it is not possible for me to mount a fair Defense without more time.

The Judge agreed with Sarah but, "I'll give you a thirty-day extension not sixty and to help, the D.A. will provide you with any materials you request swiftly, so we will not need another extension. This is a high-profile case and I want no delays. Bail is continued."

"I will need all the files, depositions, forensics, witness lists, by tomorrow morning." Sarah asked the D.A.

"No problem, the boxes are already packed," he replied confidently.

"I will also expect your help in expediting subpoenas for depositions." Sarah added.

"Of course, whatever we can do to expedite the trial is in our best interest as well."

The D.A. was extremely confident in his case. He had motive, opportunity, means and forensic evidence. In his eyes it was a slam dunk. No reason to settle out of court or delay.

Sarah knew Sterling would not intentionally kill another man but, even she was starting to question her own judgement of his innocents. Is it possible Sterling killed Broskavitch in self-defense? Also, the missing piece of what really happened in the limo that Sterling refused to share even with her, his hopefully future girlfriend, or her, his lawyer with client attorney privilege. He only shared that he would be killed if he told anyone the details of that meeting.

Sarah pushed hard for Sterling to tell her the details, but Sterling refused, "It is not that I do not trust you with what transpired; Sinski will have you killed as well if he thinks I shared any of it with you. I could not live with that."

As promised the D.A.'s office delivered almost 30 boxes of assorted papers. Nothing was organized or cataloged. The boxes were not labelled nor in chronological order. Sarah took pictures to show Judge Cullum in case she needed another extension.

Sarah called in as many friends as possible from her school days and more recent contacts. The team poured over the material and together they formulated what they felt was Sterling's best defense strategy. In short, to focus the jury on the possibility of Chapman, the jewelry store owner being the murderer, raising a reasonable doubt. Sarah knew at best this was a crap shoot defense.

Even with all these boxes, the most important reports of all, the blood DNA evidence were not fully included. Thirty-eight samples were taken on the morning within hours of the murder. Two more samples were taken the next day. All the thirty-eight samples were a positive match to Broskavitch, no one else.

But why were two more taken the next day? What did they find the next day that required more sampling? Why only two samples, why not more? Why weren't those two results back yet?

Sarah called the Prosecutor's office and asked, "for the final two DNA results."

He responded, "They are not back yet. As soon as I get them, I'll send them over. Sarah, you know that those results are not paramount to our case. If they are a match, it almost makes the case itself. Also, I have been assured that all results will be back before jury selection is complete."

Sarah petitioned the Judge in private, "Your Honor, you can see from the pictures the condition the boxes sent to us by the D.A. But most important is the incomplete DNA test. The results of that test will have an immense impact on my defense. I am going to need more time to prepare once those results are back."

"I do not want to delay this trial, but you have a valid point." answered the Judge. "Let's meet with the D.A. this afternoon. After hearing his side, I will decide if we extend the date or not. If I rule in your favor, how much time will you need? Before you answer me, that test can only match, or not match your client's DNA. You should be working on both defenses while you wait for the results. Also, your client should be able to tell you the results now, before the tests come back."

"At least a week, to be safe, two would be better." asked Sarah.

At that afternoon meeting:

"Your Honor, before we begin, I have the final DNA report for the remaining blood samples." said D.A. Brooks, handing the Judge and Sarah each an envelope. "I apologize, I gave this to my clerk to mail out, but it ended in a wrong mail basket. The results show a positive match to Mr. Russell."

Sarah was very upset but, she kept on fighting.

"How convenient," noted Sarah. "Why only two samples, not more?"

"It was a small sample, only a single drop of blood," answered D.A. Brooks.

"Why were the samples taken a whole day later?" she followed up.

"It was missed the first day because it was a very small sample and it was on the safe. Dried blood on a black safe is hard to spot, even for a forensic tech."

Judge Cullum interrupted, "I do not need to be here for this discussion. Since it will take a while for jury selection you should have plenty of time to prepare the defense. Jury selection starts Monday."

Check.

As Sarah left the courthouse she filled with tears. Her heart sank. All she could think of is that Sterling was in fact responsible for Broskavitch's death. Her eyes were so full of tears and blurred, she mis-stepped the last stair and fell to the sidewalk. Although not hurt, no one came to help her up. She felt so alone.

Sarah so needed to know how his blood got on the safe? What were the details of the fight? Did Broskavitch have a weapon? Are there any mitigating circumstances? How did Sterling even know him?

Sarah was truly afraid and sad. She knew she could lose this case and Sterling could be sent to prison for life. How is it possible she so misjudged Sterling's character?

Sarah called Sterling to her office and asked him directly, "I have just reviewed the states final forensics and know you killed Broskavitch. What I don't know is why? Were you threatened? Did he have a weapon? Why? Tell me." As she tried to hold off the tears.

Sterling was hurt. Not the sharp pain of an injury, the gut-wrenching pain of lost hope, like the final descent under water of a drowning victim. This meant Sarah both did not believe him, and thought he was capable of murdering another human. Sterling stayed silent. He could not believe what Sarah was asking.

That hurt turned to anger and he barked at Sarah; "I killed no one. Do your job and get me out of this nightmare." Sterling stamped out of the room, slamming the door behind, leaving a small trail of blood.

Sterling returned to his apartment about an hour later, and saw a notice of eviction taped to his door with a note from Manny attached, "Sorry I had to do this, but you left me no choice. You need to leave. Please read the notice and obey. Do not force me into the next steps."

More good news, thought Sterling.

Ring.... Ring.... Ring....

"Hey Sterling, it's your Dad."

"I told you last time we spoke I can not help you. I have enough problems of my own. I can not and will not help you no matter how much you owe or how they plan to hurt you," Sterling fired back.

"I know you are angry with me, but please don't hang up, I have something important to say." JR replied. "Most important, I can't begin to say how sorry I am for putting your mom in harm's way. I think of her often and it eats me up inside the injustice she suffered because of me. I also want to thank you for all your help over this past year. I know how much of a burden I have been."

"On the brighter side I signed up for Gamblers Anonymous. The group meets weekly. Part of the process includes being assigned a buddy. She is pretty cool. Her name is Katrina. And, like the storm name, she is a force not to mess with. I know it is early, but so far so good. No more bookies, no more Friday poker games. I gave my seat up to Dan, the Receiver on first shift. By not playing at the bar I also cut my beer drinking way back."

"Katrina pointed out the more you drink, the more you want to gamble. She meets me every Friday at three. Once we went to a movie. Once a walk in the park. Once bowling. Anything to keep my mind off the game," he added.

"I also wanted to tell you that Ned the Knee was found dead. Police investigated me because of the obvious motive with Lynn's murder. Good thing I was at the movies with Katrina and kept my ticket. They told me he was murdered gangland style, including both knees smashed with a bat; another reason they looked at me. They may question you now that you are back."

"Anyway, that's why I called. But I have been doing all the talking. What's new in your life? Your trial is very soon. Are you ready?"

"Let me just say it is a work in progress. I'd like to fill you in on the details but can't right now. I will call you when I can. I am proud of you for joining G.A., stay with it. Thanks for calling."

Ring.... Ring....

Who now? Thought Sterling, picking up the phone.

"I need my diamonds back. I know you stole them from the safe. I will let you keep the cash if you return the diamonds. You my even keep your precious gold cross. I must have the diamonds back. Do we have a deal?"

"Chapman, I know it's you, I know your voice." answered Sterling. "But I have no idea what you are talking about. I would love to get the cross back, but I don't know anything about any diamonds or cash." Being extra careful not admitting to any criminal activity in case of a wiretap.

"Well know this, when they come for me, and they will, I'm going to give them your name. If you want to live, give me back the diamonds and this will all go away." replied Chapman.

Sterling was not scared of Chapman's threats because Sinski already knew Sterling had given the black bag to Ned the Knee.

"Can't help you. Good bye."

Click.

CHAPTER 17

AT THE TRIAL

"As our first witness, I'd like to call the owner of the Forest Hills jewelry store, Mr. Chapman."

"Mr. Chapman, can you tell us about your relationship with the defendant Mr. Russell?"

"Yes. He is; or was my accountant assigned to me by the firm of Fine, Fine, and Ginsberg."

"Take us back to that day when you first received a phone call from Mr. Russell."

"Sterling called me and told me we were scheduled for an audit and he insisted we do an internal audit first to make sure everything was in order. I play by the rules so thought it was a good idea."

"When did the government audit take place?" asked D.A. Brooks already knowing it didn't.

"It never did. Never happened." he answered.

"So, Mr. Russell lied to you?"

"Yes."

"Objection." voiced Sarah, "no intent established."

"I'll allow it," growled an unhappy judge.

"Who would end up paying for this pre-audit?" asked Brooks.

"That would be me. Fine, Fine, and Ginsberg charge $125/ hr. for their services." Chapman answered.

"So, by doing this pre-audit the defendant generates substantial revenue for his company. Correct?"

"Yes."

"Can you think of any other reason?" Brooks asked.

"Yes. An audit is very detailed. He is looking at all my receipts, my products, and goods. It is done in the back room where the records are kept, directly across from my workbench and safe."

"Your Honor I Object!" as Sarah was interrupted by the Judge.

"Sustained. Please rephrase you question."

"Where exactly was the audit done?"

"At my desk." answered Chapman.

"Where is that in relation to the safe?" asked the D.A.

"It is across the walkway, about four feet away."

"Is the safe ever open during the audit?"

"Yes. We leave it on day lock." Chapman answered. "We go to the safe two to three times an hour, so it is not practical to lock it every time. Instead by setting it on day lock, a two-number spin will open it."

"Was the defendant ever present when you opened the safe?"

"Yes."

"Could he see the day lock numbers?"

"Not sure, but probably."

"Would it be possible for him to see what was in the safe?"

"That I am sure of, absolutely." replied Chapman.

"What was in the safe?" asked Brooks.

"Mostly jewelry, a little cash, and some papers. Only the cash and jewels were taken."

"See this list, marked exhibit 1. Is this the list you provided the insurance company of what was stolen?"

"Yes."

"According to this list there was about $25,000 in various jewelry and an undetermined amount of cash; but approximately $2,000. Is that correct?"

"Yes."

"You mentioned a gold cross to the police, tell us about it."

"Yes. It's a gold cross with five artificial diamonds. I purchased it from Mr. Russell for $500. He was desperate for money. He said his wife was soaking him in a divorce. I offered all I could, $500. I gave the police the receipt."

"Defense exhibit 2."

"So, Mr. Russell was pleased?"

"Hardly, he was angry and wanted more. He said I was cheating him. He took the $500 but was visibly upset."

"Your witness."

"Mr. Chapman," Sarah showing him the receipt again, "This says $500 was payed for the cross, but is it signed?"

"No."

"So, the defendant never signed the slip?"

"Correct."

"Why not?"

"I didn't think it was necessary. He was my accountant. It is not like I was trying to hide anything. If I was 'cooking the books', so to speak, wouldn't I make the receipt very high like $10,000. Then I'd get more insurance money or at least pay less tax."

"Isn't it true you paid Sterling $5500 for the necklace?"

"No. Not true."

"Objection, asked and answered."

"Sustained. Move on please."

"How much is the necklace truly worth?"

"Value is in the eye of the beholder. I do not want to hurt Sterling's feelings. Those stones are cubic zirconia, not diamonds. Five hundred was a generous offer. To Sterling it was worth much more because it belonged to his mother."

"So, if that cross were to be found, it is your testimony; under oath; under penalties of perjury that the necklace is worth $500?" asked Sarah.

"Yes."

"Mr. Chapman, did you know the victim, Mr. Broskavitch?"

"I didn't."

"Did you ever meet him or talk to him?"

"Never."

"No more questions at this time but we reserve the right to recall this witness at a later date."

"Next the prosecution calls Mr. Hanna from the Boston Crime Lab."

"Mr. Hanna please describe to us the evidence you uncovered at the murder scene." asked D.A. Brooks.

"First there was numerous fingerprints, Mr. Chapman's, Mr. Broskavitch's, and the defendant Mr. Russell's. That's not unusual except we found Mr. Russell's on glass from a broken clock on the floor. We also determined that the cause of death was a brain hemorrhage caused by blunt force trauma to the head. We also matched hair samples found in broken glass to that of the victim. In addition, there was no evidence of a struggle. There were no defensive wounds on his arms or knuckles. It appeared that more clocks were broken, and things pushed onto the floor to give the look of a fight. Our conclusion was that Broskavitch was hit hard in the back of the head without warning."

"Please show exhibit 3 a photo of the crime scene to the jury."

"So, are you saying Mr. Russell's fingerprints are on the murder weapon?"

"Not exactly. During the event, four of the same make and model clocks were broken; Mr. Russell's prints were on at least one of them."

"Anyone else's prints?"

"As you would expect, the store owner?"

"Any other evidence linking Mr. Russell to the crime scene?"

"Yes, blood." answered Mr. Hanna.

"Please explain."

"We have an exact match of the defendant's blood taken from a sample on the inside edge of the safe door. That sample proves Sterling was close enough to the safe for a single drop of blood to fall when the safe door was open."

"Your witness."

Check.

Sarah knew they were in trouble. She needed to put some doubt into the jury's mind. Sterling held his head down. He also knew it was pretty much over.

"You said Mr. Chapman's prints were also on the broken glass? Raising her eyebrows slightly.

"Yes, the store owner, Mr. Chapman's prints."

"So, isn't it possible that Mr. Chapman broke a clock over the victim's head?"

"Yes, it is possible."

"Based on the blood tests, when did he die?"

"About 4:30 am."

"How accurate is the timing of the blood tests?"

"Plus, or minus one hour, somewhere between 3:30 am and 5:15 am."

"So, if your test shows 4:30 am, then why would the range be from 3:30 to 5:15 am?"

"Why the odd 15 minutes?" Sarah asked.

"The first police on the scene came at 5:15 am and Broskavitch was dead then. This was a very fresh crime scene. The liver tests determined his death at about 4:30 am as well. The timing of the blood tests were not as specific because of the large amount of blood thinners in the victim's system."

"So, by your testimony, the victim could only have been murdered between 3:30 am and 5:15 am." Sarah could spin this in closing arguments using Sterling's alibi to further close the window of opportunity. She felt good about her cross examination until...

Mr. Hanna rebutted, "Not necessarily. The victim could have laid on the floor unconscious, bleeding internally for an hour or more before dying."

"Isn't it also true that all of the blood samples were not taken the same time. In fact, some were taken the next day?" Sarah asked.

"Correct, thirty-eight samples were taken with in hours of the murder, and two were taken the next day."

"Which ones had the defendant's blood on them?" Sarah asked.

"Only the two later ones. All thirty-eight from the first night matched the victim."

"Why were they done a day later?"

"They were not found the night of the murder. These were found the next day with better light. Remember, this was only a small drop of dried dark red blood on the inside edge of the black safe door. I think it is amazing we found it at all."

"How long was this blood on the safe before sampling."

"After twenty-four hours it is hard to be specific."

"I'm done for now," said Sarah as she returned to the chair. She felt good that by now no one in the jury had even a clue as to what the blood evidence did or didn't mean. Then...

"Redirect your honor?"

The Judge nodded yes.

"I'm confused. Can you tell us what this blood testing proves?"

"In short, the defendant's blood was on the inside of the safe door, and that can only happen if he is present when it was open. The prints prove that the defendant touched at least one of the four clocks that ended up broken, and one of those four clocks was the murder weapon."

Sterling saw his future, they were losing. Check.

"Next witness I call Detective Scott." said D.A. Brooks.

"When did you first suspect the defendant?"

"Chapman came to the store early that day about 5 am and found the crime scene. He called us at the station at 5:03 exactly and we responded. First patrol car arrived at 5:14 am and I met my partner Detective O'Brien there at 5:35 am. Mr. Chapman told us he thought the defendant, Mr. Russell was responsible; pointing to the defendant. He told us of his anger over the $500 Mr. Russell received for a necklace. Also, that Mr. Russell was his accountant, and he had just spent a week in the store backroom going over Chapman's books before an audit. Lastly, that his anger over the necklace was triggered by his financial problems caused by a divorce."

"What did you do next Detective?"

"I obtained a search warrant and along with Detective O'Brien drove to Mr. Russell's apartment, arriving just after 6:30 am to look for evidence."

"What kind of evidence?"

"Items taken from the safe; money, jewelry; blood stained clothes, tools used to break in. You get the idea. Most importantly to speak with the defendant about any possible alibi. The sooner after a crime the better to talk to any suspects, before they have time to change their story or to ask friends for an alibi."

"Did the defendant have an alibi?" asked the D.A."

"Only partly."

"Please explain."

"From 7 to 9 pm we have solid proof he was at home. The landlord spoke with him at 7 pm and repaired his toilet in person at 9 pm. In the middle, phone records confirmed he called clients from his landline. Paperwork on his table supports this as well. I can say without hesitation that he was home from 7 to 9 pm. After 9 pm until 6:30 am, Mr. Russell has no alibi."

Sterling could not believe his ears. His iron clad alibi worked. It worked so well it is going to get him convicted of murder.

Detective Scott's testimony went for the rest of the day. Details after details were presented. His notes and presentation style were flawless. He was credible;

sincere; a nightmare for the defense. He spent an extra amount of time in testifying about the divorce settlement, and Sterling's lost job.

Scott also linked Sterling's mother's death to an organized crime hit. However, the most damaging testimony was at the end.

"We know that Mr. Russell had motive and opportunity; but he didn't have the skills to crack open that safe. He had seen the jewelry but needed help to open the safe." stated D.A. Brooks.

"Objection." yelled Sarah. "Mr. Brooks is stating opinions."

"Sustained," said the Judge.

"What did the victim, Broskavitch, do for work?" asked Brooks.

"According to this Interpol report, he was a Russian safe cracking expert. His specialty was diamond theft. He has ties to the Russian mob and has been implicated but not charged in numerous homicides." Scott replied.

"Please enter the Interpol report as exhibit 7."

"As we see it, Broskavitch opened the safe then someone got greedy and hit him over the head with a clock."

"Objection your Honor. The prosecutor is stating facts not in evidence. There has been no evidence that the victim opened the safe."

"Sustained. Save your opinions for your closing arguments." said the Judge.

"By someone you mean the defendant?"

"Well we can't ask Broskavitch can we?" replied Detective Scott.

"Objection!"

"Sustained. Detective you know better. Pull this one more time and I will hold YOU in contempt," roared an angry Judge.

"Sorry your Honor."

"How did Mr. Russell know Broskavitch?" the D.A. asked.

"We don't know for sure, but we do know that both the victim and the accused share a common connection. Broskavitch worked for Derek Sinski, a senior member of the Russian mob. The defendant's $250,000 bail was paid in full, no bond, by Derek Sinski. Immediately after Mr. Russell's release, he entered Sinski's limo and met with him for almost ten minutes."

"Did you take this picture?" asked Brooks holding up a large photo.

"Yes. It's our favorite. Doesn't that ear to ear smile tell it all."

"Please mark exhibit 8 and show the jury."

Check.

Sarah was able to water down some of the Detective's testimony, but the damage was done. The prosecution was on target for a conviction.

Drip.

Sterling felt it coming and turned his head quickly. The drop of blood landed about mid table from him. It sparkled from the courthouse lights against the polished oak wooden table. As usual Sterling went for his handkerchief, until Sarah yelled, "STOP!" Sterling froze in place.

"Your Honor, for the record, Mr. Russell just experienced a very small nose bleed at 4:03 pm, just a single drop. This is a medical condition caused by an increase in blood pressure when under duress combined with thin walled capillaries in his nose. A condition Mr. Russell has had his entire life. That statement will be supported by evidence of medical records during the defense. I see Mr. Hanna of the crime lab is still in court, could you instruct him to sample the blood and to measure the distance it traveled before hitting the table?"

"So ordered. Mr. Hanna do your thing. We'll resume court tomorrow at 9 am. Court's adjourned."

CHAPTER 18

THE TRUTH

"Sterling, we need to talk, now," said Sarah in a concerned voice. "Let's go to my office."

"Oh this A.C. unit never works on the hot days." As she took off her suit coat exposing a white blouse. Sterling immediately noticed the two top buttons were undone exposing her black bra.

"They nailed you pretty good," said Sarah.

"Motive-Desperate for money/divorce."

"Opportunity-Your blood inside the safe."

"Your Fingerprints – On the possible murder weapon."

"No Alibi-After 9 pm."

"Mob Connections-Long history with Russian Mob."

"Mother's murder gangland style."

"Father's gambling troubles."

"Quarter million in bail money."

"Stunning photo with a smile."

"You need to talk to me and do it now. I cannot defend you if you lie to me or hold back. The D.A. isn't going to cut a deal; he has no need."

"I didn't kill Broskavitch. You have my word. I am not a killer. You must believe me. It's important to me that you do," replied Sterling.

"Well explain how the blood got inside the safe. I guessed at the court that it was a single drop from your nose given the size of the sample. But how did it get on the edge of the open door?"

"When I robbed the safe. I had trouble with the combination. I must have tried it twenty times before it finally opened. I felt ready to explode when it finally released. The blood drop had to happen when I swung the door open for it to be on the edge. It was the perfect crime except for a single drop of blood."

"So, when were you there?"

"8 pm."

"Stop lying. The police proved you were home from 7-9 pm." voiced Sarah with anger and despair.

"Because I wanted them to." replied Sterling. "I broke the toilet when I got back so the landlord would see me at 9 pm. I broke a clock in the store to establish the time of the robbery at 8 pm. Why didn't the crime lab find that? I used a phone calling system to make robo calls to two clients I knew were out of town, I'm their accountant. By not leaving a message they can only trace the calls via the phone company records. Which they did."

"Where is the phone equipment?"

"Gone. I set up a Dump Bag. Equipment, my clothes, the webcam and anything even remotely connected to the heist went into the bag. That bag went out for trash pickup with all the others about 9 pm the night of the robbery." answered Sterling.

"No prints on your entry of climbing through the broken window, so you used gloves, but why prints on the clock?" she asked.

"When I first came to work there, the desk I was going to use had six clocks on it. I helped Chapman move them. Speaking of gloves, if I wore gloves, how would my prints end up on the clock? I wouldn't take them off just BEFORE I killed someone, then put them back on before I climbed out the window. Makes no sense; shows those prints were from before."

"Chapman killed Broskavitch." added Sterling. "First, he has been lying. He gave me $5500, not $500 for the cross."

"Why would he say that?" Sarah asked.

"To give me motive. He set me up; 'I have been cheated, I am angry' he said in court. He lied about the audit. I never said it was 'scheduled'. I told him the IRS is focusing on independent jewelers."

"OK, how did you open the safe?"

"I set up a small webcam. In fact, at the trial Chapman said that, 'possibly I could have seen the numbers.' No way. They were almost invisible that safe is so old. I had to spill a little white out on the dial to get a bearing on the numbers. Check it out, the whiteout is still on the dial."

"And the mob connection?"

"My father has a serious gambling problem. It is the reason my mother was murdered. It is why I robbed the store in the first place. Unless I payed a gangster known as Ned the Knee $40,000, he would kill my father like he did my mother."

"The Russian, I had never met until that day when I was escorted by two men to the limo. Apparently, Chapman was fronting jewelry for this person Derek. I did not know it, I just saw a sealed black cloth bag in the safe and figured it would be valuable."

"Sterling, you best option is to confess to the robbery and what you just told me. However, they will not believe you. They will say you are saying this to just save yourself. You will need to give back the jewels."

"I can't. I gave the bag unopened to Ned as payment for my Dad's debt. If I go to the police Derek will have me killed."

"He threatened you in the limo?"

"Never directly. But, read between the lines. I am shuffled into a bullet proof limo by two huge men. The person I do not know, just posted $250,000 cash for my bail. He wanted to know what I did with his bag of jewels. I told him I gave them to Ned the Knee in New Jersey to pay off my Dad's debt. He told me not to skip bail, he has a long reach. He didn't have to threaten me, I know what is at stake."

"I need a moment to sort this all out." As she sat on a chair, Sterling noticed the rosiness of her cheeks. She was hot with passion over this case.

"Chapman must have met Broskavitch in the store to pick up the jewels and found the safe empty. Chapman must have killed him rather than face Derek," said Sterling.

"I still do have the cash. Chapman said $2000, I put $40,000 in one locker and the rest, about $15,000 in a separate locker. I can give the police that money."

"Not yet, $55,000 smells of mob, not until we have a strategy and plan." Sarah answered.

Sterling loved those two words. It was like playing a chess game and it was part of Sarah's nature. His feelings for Sarah kept growing.

Sarah and Sterling spent most of the night working together on the next day's strategy. The best plan was still to give the jury a plausible alternative to the murderer. Recall each witness and point all leads toward Chapman. Give the jury reasonable doubt. It would be a huge risk. The Judge may not even let Sarah proceed. Sarah and Sterling worked until 2 am. Sterling went home and found his apartment locks changed.

Drip.

He slept a few hours in the hallway.

CHAPTER 19

THE DEFENSE

"The Defense recalls Mr. Hanna from the Boston Crime Lab. And as a reminder you are still under oath." explained Sarah.

"Were you able to determine how the store was broken into? How did someone enter?"

"Yes. They broke a small window in the back room that looks into the service alley where deliveries come, dumpsters reside, you get the idea," he answered.

"Is there any other way of entry?" Sarah asked.

"No."

"How about the front door?" exclaimed Sarah.

"No. We ruled it out, and other windows; no pry marks or breakage on any of them. Also, the glass was broken from the alley into the store. Almost all the broken glass was inside, not in the alley."

"Were there any fingerprints on the window or glass?"

"No."

"Wouldn't someone have to pull themselves up and through the window to get in?"

"Yes."

"You said it was a small window, so again why no prints?" asked Sarah.

"Gloves."

"So, you believe the criminal used gloves?"

"Yes, otherwise we would have found prints."

"Did you find Broskavitch's fingerprints on the window, the front door, or the safe door?"

"No. Besides we did measurements and it was not possible for Broskavitch to even fit through that small of a window, but Mr. Russell could. Broskavitch was let in through the front door. No prints of his on the safe either."

"Did you find Mr. Russell's fingerprints on the window, the front door, or the safe door?"

"No, his prints were only on the broken glass from a clock."

"Your honor if you would allow me some leeway, I'd like to roleplay what Mr. Hanna is telling us. I promise you it will be short."

"I'll allow it but be very careful."

Sarah took a pair of vinyl gloves from her pocket and put them on.

"So, I come to the window in the alley with my gloves on and smash the window," waving her arms. "Next I crawl through the broken window into the store," raising her arms pretending to pull herself up. "Cut the alarm and let Broskavitch in the front door, who opens the safe. I take off my gloves," raising her eyes in surprised look, "then pick up a clock and hit the victim in the back of the head," making appropriate arm swings.

"Now I put my gloves back on (fighting with the once removed gloves) so to not leave fingerprints on the door or window when I leave."

"Objection, gloves aren't necessary to not leave fingerprints in opening a door. Use a shirt tail to turn the knob."

"Sustained."

"Mr. Hanna, even if the gloves stayed off, as an experienced evidence investigator does it make sense to you that a criminal would remove their gloves prior to committing an assault? Wouldn't they complete the crime before removing the gloves?"

"Usually."

"Isn't it possible that the fingerprints on the clock glass came from picking it up a few days earlier, say when the Defendant started doing the audit in the back room?"

"Yes, that is possible."

"Mr. Hanna, you said the prints on the safe were Chapman's, on the clocks were Chapman's, on the alarm horn were Chapman's. Isn't another way into the store through the front door; with a key?" Sarah asked loudly.

"Yes."

"Couldn't the broken window from the alley be a simple staging to make it look like a break-in?"

"That's possible."

"Now let's talk about the blood. You witnessed Sterling's single drop of blood at trial and measured the distance it traveled, correct?" Changing topics.

"Yes, twenty-two inches." Replied Mr. Hanna

"If he were standing would it have travelled further?" asked Sarah.

"Yes, by my calculation, up to twenty-nine inches away."

"Did you have time to review the medical records we provided about his nosebleed condition?"

"Yes. I reviewed it with our medical staff and it concludes he has a condition that can release a small amount of blood from his nose, if his blood pressure gets too high. And, he has had it all his life."

"As previously stated by Mr. Chapman, the store owner, the safe was four feet across an aisle from the table where sterling performed the audit. When the safe door was swung open, it would extend into the aisle how far?"

"Just short of half way, twenty-four inches is the width of the safe door, and the distance from the desk to the safe is forty-nine inches." Hanna answered.

"Prior testimony from Mr. Chapman said that Mr. Russell could see the contents of the safe, meaning the door was open with Mr. Russell present. Given that the drop of blood range of travel is between twenty-two inches sitting and twenty-nine inches if standing, the open safe door being twenty-five inches away is in range from the desk. Correct?"

"Based on only that one sample, I guess so." answered Mr. Hanna reluctantly.

"So, Mr. Hanna, you said earlier, that you could not be specific about when the blood droplet that matched the Defendant's fell onto the safe. So, isn't it possible that Mr. Russell had a small nose bleed when the safe door was open under day lock, with the store owner present; say the day before?"

"Ya."

"I'm sorry, please speak up, the jury couldn't hear you."

"YES." spoken loudly.

Sarah felt great. She had established doubt over the fingerprints and the blood samples on the safe. Doing the same with the police was next.

"I recall Detective Scott," said Sarah.

"Please explain the evidence you have that connects Mr. Russell with the victim." asked Sarah.

"I don't understand." replied Detective Scott.

"You testified that the two of them, Russell and Broskavitch, broke in together and robbed the safe. What physical evidence supports this claim? Phone records, witness that saw them together, recordings from security cameras?"

"Isn't it true that you connected Broskavitch with Sinski but never connected him to the Defendant?"

"No. They both knew Sinski." yelled back Scott.

Sarah rebuffed, "So I know the Judge and you know the Judge, then we must be in cahoots?"

"Sinski didn't risk $250,000 bail money for nothing," countered Detective Scott.

"Then let me ask you, why did he?" asked Sarah

"I don't know why, but he did."

Sarah made her point that much of Scott's testimony was not backed up by evidence. But he drove home the Russian connection of a quarter million dollars that did hurt the defense significantly.

"The Defense recalls Mr. Chapman."

"Again, the Defense recalls Mr. Chapman."

"Your Honor, may we approach?" asked the D.A.

"Yes."

"Mr. Chapman is in the missing. He was due in court an hour ago. We checked his house and store but have not located him yet."

"Your Honor, Chapman knew he was supposed to be in court today and when. It's obvious, he is running." Sarah yelled, bursting with new hope.

"Nonsense," replied the D.A., "We just don't know where he is. He could be on the side of the highway with a flat tire for all we know."

"If he is not located by noon, I'll issue a bench warrant. In the mean time call your next witness," ordered Judge Cullum.

"The Defense calls Officer O'Brien." Sarah was hoping to derail O'Brien. Being a hot head could help cast doubt on Detective Scott's testimony.

"That's Detective O'Brien, Missy"

"Missy? Excuse me!"

"Stop this." As the Judge slammed his mallet adding, "I expect you both to act as professionals."

Even with a good start, Sarah was not able to undo the harm of Scott's testimony about the bail money.

Before completing her questions, the Judge received a paper from the clerk. It informed the Judge that Chapman was in the Boston City Hospital I.C.U. He was unconscious and missing two fingers.

"Court is adjourned for today. I'll see both attorneys in my chambers immediately."

In the chambers, "Have a seat please," said the Judge.

"Here is what we know. Chapman is in the I.C.U. They have given him 50/50 odds of surviving. He is unconscious and is missing two fingers."

"Oh my God," said Sarah.

"He was found in the alley one street over from his store."

"Your Honor, I ask for a mistrial. He is a key witness. This shows he is the one connected to the Russian mob, not my client. Fingers missing is torture, that's revenge, not just some random mugging." asked Sarah almost pleading.

"No. Sorry. Not yet," replied the Judge.

"Any comments from the People?" he asked.

"Just one. I'd like to Know where Mr. Russell was last night and this morning?"

"He was with me until after 2 am," answered Sarah.

"Really!" said the D.A. with eyebrows raised.

"Yes, working on today's questions," she rebuffed.

"Enough," said the Judge. "We'll recess for three days to allow the police time to sort out what happened. We will meet in chambers at 9 am Friday. I want the police report no later than noon Thursday. I'll decide then about a mistrial."

When Sarah told Sterling all he could think about was being able to spend 3 more days of freedom hopefully spending that time with Sarah.

CHAPTER 20

CHAPMAN RECOVERS

Chapman survived and was more than ready to tell all about Derek Sinski. He was petrified. He knew he was left for dead and was supposed to have been killed. He knew he would be killed. He knew he would be killed as soon as released, possibly even while in the hospital.

"I want to speak to the FBI," said Chapman.

"No, you'll speak to us," said Detective O'Brien.

"I can give you Derek Sinski. Head of the Boston Russian mob; but I want a deal first and I want it with the FBI not with the Boston Police Department."

"How about we just let the word out you're alive?"

"Nurse, hand me that phone, I'll call the FBI myself."

"Fine, we'll bring in the FBI. In the mean time, who did this to you? Was it Sterling Russell?"

"That Wuss! No. But that SOB did rob my store. He is the reason I am in this mess in the first place. Yeah, on second thought he's the one that did this to me."

Several hours later Special Agent Clark walks in with Detective O'Brien.

"Mr. Chapman; this is Special Agent Clark from the FBI's organized crime unit. You have something to tell him?"

"Yeah, but here's the deal. First, full immunity for all crimes related in any way to the Russian mob. Second, witness protection. House, job at a jeweler's, and in writing. I'll give you Sinski and the whole diamond smuggling game."

"Agreed, provided you testify in court and have something valuable to say. Now, what happened?"

Chapman told the FBI about the jewels.

"I'd receive a shipment of uncut diamonds in anniversary clocks sent from Russia, the type that has a large glass dome over the actual clock-works. Inside the bottom was a hidden compartment. The base of each clock looked like marble. It is a very hard granate. Like what you would see on a new kitchen counter. The diamonds were placed in the hollow and suspended in a wax."

"The plate that holds the clock mechanism is attached over the hole. X-rays at customs would show the bottom solid with small stones throughout, consistent with granate. Likewise, without suspicion the customs people are reluctant to remove the glass and take off the actual clock works."

"Clocks were shipped twelve in a case. Each clock held $20,000 worth of diamonds."

"My job was to take off the clock and remove the wax and diamonds. Melt the wax off and recover the gems. I would give them to Broskavitch and he would pay me $7,000 cash per case."

"What then happened to the diamonds?" asked Agent Clark.

"I have no idea."

"What happened to the clocks?"

"I sold them to my special clients."

"Like who?"

"Usually, street people wanting to hide drugs. The clocks keep very poor time."

"What happened that night?" asked Agent Clark.

"As usual I met Broskavitch at the store at 4:30 am. As soon as I entered the store, I knew there was a problem. The alarm panel was tripped, and the horn wire was cut."

"I went immediately to the safe and sure enough the door was open; the diamonds and cash gone!"

"Anything else?"

"Yes, a single clock was smashed as well as the alley window. I knew right away that it had to be Russell, my accountant. He is a thief and you should arrest him."

"Keep going," said Clark.

"Broskavitch was right behind me. I knew what was going to happen to me. Derek would require me to pay back the $240,000 or he would have me killed."

"I said to Broskavitch, 'My God, I've been robbed. You must tell Derek. This was not my fault. Tell him it must have been my accountant at Fine, Fine and

Ginsberg. Yes, he must have taken them out of the safe."

"No, you tell him yourself. I do not believe a man as smart as you would hide such a valuable treasure in such an old safe. I think you hid them and set this up."

"With that he started to reach for his gun. I knew that meant certain death. I jumped at him and we fell over the desk. I reached out, grabbed a clock, and hit him in the back of the head. I broke more clocks, waited until 5 am, and then called the police."

"What happened after that?"

"Yesterday morning Derek's men found me. They were ruthless. They kept hitting me and kicking me. Then they sat me up and cut off two of my fingers with pruning shears. Next thing I remember is being here in the hospital."

"Could you identify them?"

"Even, if I could, I wouldn't. They would find me and kill me. He has connections everywhere. I testify at his trial then go straight into witness protection from the court house.

Wednesday PM at the DA's office.

"Mr. Clark and Mr. Brooks, you asked to meet with me about a possible plea deal with my client Mr. Russell." said Sarah.

"Yes, we have new information and would like to discuss a settlement," replied Brooks.

"New information; by law you must turn it over to me," said Sarah.

"It's sealed by Federal Court order. However, we know Sterling stole from the store. We are not 100% sure of the murder. So, we are willing to drop the Murder charge, if he confesses to the Burglary."

"Oh cute," responded Sarah. "What Burglary are you speaking of? The list produced by Mr. Chapman? I am sure his insurance company is paying on his 'say so' as well. He has no credibility now. I don't think there even was a theft!"

"Oh, you're good Sarah, but we can we still have a strong case. And we're not going to be embarrassed," said Brooks.

"We'll accept Unarmed Burglary: Misdemeanor, three to six months, at Gardner Prison," threw out Sarah, not expecting them to bite.

"Agreed, providing Mr. Russell is disposed by us and agrees to testify in Federal Court. We have enough to take down the entire Russian diamond operation but need collaborating testimony."

Sarah added," But, if he has no collaborating testimony, he still gets the deal."

D.A. Brooks answered, "Yes, provided he tells us about the limo meeting, or the deals off."

"Let me check with my client, and I'll call you later today. I think he will agree."

Sarah explained the deal to Sterling but, she didn't get the reaction she expected. Sterling was scared and said a flat out, "NO, I will not testify in court against Derek Sinski. Under no circumstances will I testify. Derek will kill you, me, your mother, my dad, and others if he has any idea that I would testify in court against him. Sarah you can't let this happen."

Sarah saw how afraid Sterling was of Derek. "You know, I feel we can beat the murder wrap, but you will be in jail a long time for even a reduced charge to Burglary One with out this plea deal. You will also lose your career being convicted of a Felony. We're talking a long list of charges that will end up with a sentence over a decade long. They will also put you in the worst possible prison they can; a cell and inmates more like your fist night before I met you in Boston. Three to six months at Gardner Prison is a gift, you should take it."

"It's not a gift if you are dead in three to six months and one day," countered Sterling.

"Sterling, you told me you had nothing to do with this whole Russian mob connection so, what can you say that would help the Feds? What can you collaborate?"

"Nothing. But just the fact that I would testify is enough to put us all in danger."

Sarah suggested, "Let me try this. Let me ask you the questions I think the prosecutors will ask, and you tell the truth. Let's see what is exposed."

"When did you first see the diamonds?" asked Sarah.

"I never saw a diamond except those in display cases of the store."

"What about the diamonds in the black bag?"

"I never opened the black bag, it was sealed."

"When holding the bag, didn't it feel like a lot of diamonds?"

"I don't know what a bag of diamonds feels like. I thought it was jewelry like a pearl necklace or ear rings."

"Let's stop for one minute. Do you know what time it is," Sarah asked?

"2:30" he answered.

"That's not what I asked you. I asked you if you <u>knew</u> what time it was. The answer is 'yes'. Go back to the previous question about holding the black bag, if you answered no; that's perfect. Don't add what you thought, or about pearls. Just no. Make them ask the question. Don't volunteer anything extra."

Sarah continued, "In the limo, Did Sinski bring up the diamonds?"

"No."

"Did he even once use the word diamond."

"No."

"Did he ask you about the black bag."

"Yes."

"What did he ask?"

"What I did with it."

"What did you do with it?"

"I put the sealed bag in a bus locker and mailed the key to a P.O. Box in New Jersey to pay off a gambling debt."

"What was his name?"

"Ned. I don't know his last name."

"What box and city?"

"I don't remember the box number, it was very long. The city was Woodbridge."

"Did Sinski threaten you?"

"No."

Sarah jumped in, "Stop. You told me we would all be killed, now you say he didn't threaten you. Which is it? You can not lie in a deposition."

"He never <u>threatened</u> me. He didn't have to, it was obvious."

"Why did he post your bail?"

"I don't know, ask him."

Sarah continued for over an hour asking questions she would ask if she was the prosecutor. There was really nothing dangerous in his testimony. The key now is to get Sinski to know that.

Sterling, thinking of chess, had a radical and highly dangerous suggestion. "What if you approach the law firm that Sinski uses and ask them to act as Second Chair. Let them dispose me at their office to show I really can't hurt them. If they say no, I reject the plea and we go back to court. If not, they can then sit in on the real deposition. If that goes bad, they give me a signal and I stop talking immediately."

"Sterling, you really believe we are in that much danger?" asked Sarah. "I would hate to see you go to prison for fifteen or more years with only three to six months being offered."

"But it would not be a happy life. Always looking over the shoulder, always concerned for our friends and relatives. I'd rather do the fifteen years myself than put you and others in danger." Sterling said bravely.

Sarah added with great emotion, "You know I have strong feelings for you, and believe you feel the same toward me. But I can't wait fifteen or more years for my life to start. If you lose, you also lose me."

A short prison stay, Sarah and probable death for both; or a long prison stay, no Sarah and a long life.

Drip.

CHAPTER 21

SECOND CHAIR

Sarah looked up previous trials involving Derek Sinski. All recent activity was handled by the law firm of "Pembroke Law." Without an appointment, Sarah asked, "I'd to see the lawyer that handles Mr. Sinski's affairs, it was a matter of great importance."

The office was on the 23rd floor of the Pru. Spacious rooms with large glass windows overlooking the Back Bay and Charles River. The office felt sterile. Cold grey cloth walls with large paintings reminding her more of a daycare than a law office, just broad swatches of color. Sarah was not impressed.

"Hello, my name is Martin Pembroke, attorney for Mr. Sinski. Please come into my office."

The room was a very large corner office with rich leather seats, marble top credenza, a large walnut desk. To the left was a large conference room, bathroom with shower and closet, and a kitchenette complete with bar. Sarah was impressed.

"Why are you here?" he asked.

"I represent Sterling Russell in ..."

"Yes, I know. I have been following the case Sarah. You have been doing a fine job in disproving the Prosecutions allegations' he murdered Broskavitch. The robbery is not so easy, that tricky bail money issue and no alibi." said Pembroke.

Sarah was dumbfounded that the owner of one of the most prestigious law firms in the city new her name and so many details of the case.

"How can I help you?" he asked.

"My client has been offered a great plea deal from the prosecutor provided he is disposed by him and agrees to testify if needed at a trial."

"And, your telling me this! You know who Mr. Sinski is and what he does? Why would you possibly tell me this?"

"Mr. Russell is very concerned for his safety. I disposed him in detail myself and he is telling the truth, and there is no reason to fear what he says. He never saw a single diamond. He never was threatened. He knows nothing of Chapman or Broskavitch. Mr. Sinski never once mentioned diamonds in the limo, only a black bag."

"But look. I know you can not just take my word for it, so we'd like to hire your firm as a Second Chair. To prepare him for the deposition, you can ask him any question and see how he would answer. When you are done, you decide if he is OK to take the plea deal or not. If you say no, we continue with the trial and turn down the plea deal. I believe you will agree with me and not see him as a threat. But you have a second chance at the deposition itself. Click your pen twice and I stop the deposition immediately and he takes the 5th."

"Gutsy, very gutsy." replied Pembroke slowly, "And, I like gutsy. I may be interested in hiring you when this is over. We're not used to Second Chair but, I will enjoy this. OK, you may have a lawyer. Bring him in tonight about 7 pm."

Mr. Pembroke himself asked the questions. He stopped asking at 10 pm. He was satisfied that Sterling was telling the truth and more importantly had no damaging testimony he could give the Prosecution. Mr. Sinski and another lawyer sat behind a one-way mirror and watched the entire process. Sinski liked Sterling because he kept his word on the bail and told him the truth about the black bag. Derek felt he could trust Sterling's word.

Mr. Pembroke disappeared into a hidden door, for a moment and returned saying, "Yes, you did well; you may take the plea. And remember, you do not want to change your answers at the real deposition. I want you both to meet Mr. Carlson or should I say meet again. You saw him at Bow Lake. He asked you at the beach if you were staying on the lake."

"Mr. Carlson has been watching from another room. He is a new attorney for our firm and will be your Second Chair. He is unknown to this area and to the people you will be dealing with. His presence will not draw suspicion. He will not speak, only hand you notes, and if need be, double click the pen. You understand what I am saying?"

"We do." said Sarah and Sterling in unison. It sounded like a marriage vow. In many ways it was.

CHAPTER 22

THE FEDERAL DEPOSITION

The Federal deposition was very intimidating to Sterling. It was held in the F.B.I.'s office on the third floor. Upon entering the building, Sarah, Sterling and Mr. Carlson all went through a metal detector, had their bags thoroughly searched, and were even patted down for weapons. They were given badges to wear on a neck strap that showed a large V for visitor, and a large 3 meaning only allowed on the third floor, all other access denied.

The hallways to the room were narrow and windowless. There were countless lefts and rights and two doors that required a pin code to unlock. Even the pictures on the hall walls were of criminals they caught, in jail with large captions below the photo: EVANS, NOW SERVING 5YRS. LYING TO THE FBI. DELMAN, NOW SERVING 20 YEARS. KIDNAPPING.

The journey to the meeting room took them past at least a dozen of these trophies.

Even the meeting room itself was uncomfortable. The room was very small as was the table, and chairs. It was warm when they entered, and the temperature rose quickly with the added people. There were no windows or air conditioning, not even water provided.

The tactic did not work on Sarah or Carlson. Although Sterling looked OK, his nose did drop blood on S.A. Clark's chair.

S.A. Clark led in with, "The meeting is being recorded," then the date and time, it was for the deposition of Sterling Russell, and had each person give their name, title and address for the record. Each did. Mr. Carlson said he was hired to assist Ms. Murray as a Second Chair and as he is new to the case, he would not be speaking, just listening. Clark then placed Sterling under oath.

Clark never asked Carlson any other follow up questions, not even the name of the law firm where he worked.

Clark started, "Mr. Russell, I want you to know that we already have done depositions with others and know all about the diamond smuggling operation with the clocks. Normally we would not share this information, but I decided to because, I cannot emphasize enough, that you do not lie to me. If you lie, I will know it. If you lie, the plea deal is off. If you lie, you will also serve an additional term in a Federal Penitentiary for at least 5 years."

"Objection. For the record, the Prosecutor is trying to intimidate Mr. Sterling."

"OK, you have been warned. First question, please tell us about the diamonds you stole from the safe."

"I do not know of any diamonds stolen from the safe."

"So, we're going to do this the hard way. Did you rob the safe at the Forest Hills Jewelry store?"

"Yes." Sterling answered.

"For the record," interjected Sarah, "his answer and any other admissions to the Burglary cannot be released to the public, nor used in any trial of the future should the plea deal not go through. These terms are stated on page 3 of that deal."

"What did you take from the safe that night?"

"My mother's cross, a stack of cash, and a sealed black cloth bag." replied Sterling.

"First question and you already lied." smirked Clark.

"Objection," yelled Sarah.

"Oh, he lied alright. His mother's cross contains 5 diamonds. He said he never saw a diamond, I believe that is lying." Still smirking.

"Really. Mr. Chapman, a jeweler by trade, under oath, told Sterling and the Court on the first day of trial that they were NOT diamonds. They were cubic zirconia stones." answered back Sarah.

"But that night he thought they were diamonds," fired back Clark.

"You didn't ask him what he thought that night. You asked, 'tell us about the diamonds stolen from the safe.' He did not lie. Also, the stones in the cross are not important to your case. This is just a means to trick my client and make him believe he will lose the plea deal if he doesn't say what you want him to say. This is a cheap shot, and you owe my client an apology."

Carlson was impressed. Part of his hidden agenda was to also evaluate Sarah for a possible lawyer position for Mr. Pembroke.

"Let me rephrase the question, understanding you are not a jeweler, and other than the cross; did you see anything that looked like it might be a diamond?"

"No, nothing." answered Sterling.

"Were there diamonds in the black bag?" asked Clark.

"I don't know. I never opened the bag."

"Not even once? Weren't you curious?"

Sterling replied answering much to broadly, "of course I was curious. But I had a plan that required specific timing. I could not delay and open the bag just to see what was in it. It was a sealed cloth bag in a jewelry store, in its' safe. I assumed it would be valuable and I could open it up later."

"Great, it is now later, what did you find when you did open the bag?" asked Clark.

"I never got to open it."

"Do you still have the bag?" asked Clark.

"No."

"Did you leave the store with the bag?"

"Yes."

"Where did you stash it?"

"In a bus terminal locker."

"And you never went back to get it?"

"Correct."

"Why not?"

"I was afraid the police might be following me."

"So, it's still in the locker?"

"I don't think so."

"Help me understand, if you put the bag in the locker after the theft, and you never took it out, why wouldn't it still be there?"

"The only reason I robbed the safe in the first place was to pay off a $40,000 debt my father owed to a gangster in New Jersey. That person threatened to kill my father and me if I didn't. Although it was never proven, that person also had my mother killed recently. He is known as Ned the Knee. I don't know his last name."

"The cash I took from the safe was mixed bills. I had no idea how much I took and certainly could not count it with the police constantly around. I also guessed the bag had some sort of jewels coming from a jewelry store. I have no way of cashing in or fencing jewels. Giving them to Ned solved both problems."

"I mailed the locker key and number along with the bus terminal address to a P.O. Box in Woodbridge, New Jersey. I don't remember the box no. but it was 7 digits. I hoped whatever was in the bag would be worth enough to pay off the debt. Since he never called again, I guessed it did."

"Like I said, I never opened the bag. I never saw what was in the bag."

Clark asked, "How do I reach this Ned person?"

"I don't know his contact information; besides I was told..."

Sarah instantly jumping in, "Objection, hearsay."

The state D.A. Brooks jumped in, "If all that is true you can produce the $2000 and the gold cross Mr. Chapman reported you stole from his safe?"

"Yes."

This same line of testimony continued for more than hour mostly by D.A. Brooks. Sterling bit by bit revealed his detailed planning and execution of an almost perfect crime. How he established the alibi, learned the safe combination, and how to silence the alarm horn. He expressed disappointment that the crime lab never mentioned the one clock Sterling broke at 8 pm to establish the time of the break-in.

S.A. Clark announced, "Let's take a fifteen-minute break. Restrooms are one the right. Water bottles are on the table outside." All members of the State and Federal Prosecutors left immediately.

Sterling started to ask Sarah, "How..."

She stopped him cold and passed a small written note that said, 'good job. Say nothing. Room is bugged with hidden cameras, and audio. Remember what time is it? Pass note to Carlson.' They each took turns using the restrooms and grabbing water. They then sat silently.

In the Prosecutor's room, it was chaos. The state D.A. Brooks could not believe his ears. The level of planning and execution from a first-time crook. He believed every word Sterling spoke, starting from the motive of the theft. He just didn't get the bail money Sinski risked if there wasn't a mob connection. That was to be addressed after the break.

S.A. Clark pointed to an agent and said, "Contact the Woodbridge FBI office and find out all you can about this Ned the Knee." He then started ranting, "we've got nothing so far. Zero connection to Chapman's diamonds. Zero connection to Broskavitch. Zero connection to Derek Sinski. Robbed the safe but never saw a diamond. We need to press him extra hard about the limo meeting and bail."

Clark then asked the field agent monitoring the room, "What was said with us all gone?"

"Nothing. A small note was pass around, that's all. One at a time they went to the restrooms and grabbed a water. I couldn't read what the note said but it was only a few words."

"Did they throw it in the trash barrel?"

"No such luck. The silent lawyer put it in his case."

"The Deposition of Sterling Russell now continues."

"Mr. Russell, isn't it true, Mr. Sinski paid your bail of $250,000 cash?"

"Yes."

Sterling was immediately pleased that the D.A.s had changed topics. They never asked any more questions about the money or cross.

"Why do you think he would risk a quarter of a million dollars on you showing up to court?"

"I do not know." answered Sterling.

"Where had you met Mr. Sinski before?"

"I never had met him before that day."

"Did you ever work for Sinski in any way including as an accountant maybe?"

"No. Never."

"For one of his many companies?"

"No. Look at my client list. It is very short at Fine, Fine, and Ginsberg. I do not believe any of them are owned by Mr. Sinski." answered Sterling.

"We've done that already. I'm talking about the after-hours book keeping. The not reported book keeping jobs."

Mr. Carlson took out his pen and a pad of paper. He clicked the pen once. A warning.

"I would never chance my Certifications for something like that. Never. The work I do is above board and honest," replied an agitated Sterling.

"Yes honest, like stealing from a safe." countered Clark. "How about Chapman's books. Were there any irregularities in his books."

"None that I found."

"To continue, did you meet with Mr. Sinski after you were released on bail?"

"Yes, in a limo."

Sarah whispered in his ear, "make them ask the question, do not give out extra information, like in a limo."

"Did he ask you about the diamonds?" asked Clark.

"No."

"Did he ever once say the word diamonds."

"No."

"So why did Sinski want to see you."

One pen click.

He wanted my assurance that I would not skip bail. It was a lot of money and he wanted me to understand the importance of not running."

"So, he threatened you?"

"No. He never threatened me."

"Why would he risk such a large amount of cash on you. What is in it for him?"

Sterling answered. "I don't know. I don't care, it saved me from rotting in jail before the trial, and I just said thank you."

Clark continued for another half hour but was not able to change Sterling's position.

Carlson put his pen in his pocket.

D.A. Clark said in an angry voice, "Your telling us, you never once saw a single diamond, not in the safe, not in the black bag?"

"Correct."

"You never talked to Sinski nor Sinski to you about diamonds?"

"Correct."

"That Sinski never threatened you?"

"Correct."

"That from a professional CPA, Chapman's books are squeaky clean?"

"Well, squeaky clean isn't a professional accounting term; but I found no irregularities.

"Mr. Brooks, any more questions from the state?"

"No."

"We're done. Thank you for coming. You'll get a copy of the transcript in 3 days. Review it, then sign the release. If anything is wrong with it, call my office so we can correct it quickly. The agent will take your badges and show you to the door," said a very disappointed and frustrated Clark.

Sarah jumped in, "Before we go, Mr. Brooks, can I assume this testimony completes the states condition for a deposition as one of the conditions of the plea deal?"

"Yes, provided he turns in the $2000 and the cross to prove his story. See me in my office Thursday with the items, about 10 am."

"10 am it is."

Outside the FBI building Carlson complimented Sarah on the fine job she had done prepping Sterling for the deposition.

"The preparation was simple, a few rules all of us lawyers follow in depositions. Sterling just told the truth. The nice thing about the truth is that when asked a second or third time it doesn't change. Sterling is no threat to your boss."

She added, "Even if Chapman was somehow involved, it would only be with the now deceased Broskavitch, not with Sinski. This will never make trial in my eyes."

Carlson knew Chapman was in a safe house. He smiled oddly at Sarah and responded, "I agree, this will never make trial."

Sarah left with a very uneasy feeling in her gut. What exactly did that mean!

CHAPTER 23

THE FED CASE FOLDS

Sarah took Sterling to her apartment. They stopped to pick up some basic items, like clothes and toiletries. After sharing the cabin in the scout camp last July, Sarah was fine letting Sterling stay with her, but she insisted he sleep on a cot in the living room at least until the case is over. Should the plea deal fall apart, and Sterling end up with a long prison sentence, she did not want to be overly committed to the relationship. Sterling called his father.

Ring.... Ring.... Ring....

"Hi, Dad," Sterling said as soon as JR answered the phone.

"Hi Sterling," answered his dad.

"Just calling to see how you're doing."

"Fine, just fine. In fact, I was going to call you with some good news. My company was just bought out by KRRK, some financial group out of California. They're afraid of us all leaving so they gave us $2,000 bonus if we stay another month and another $2,000 bonus if we remain 13 weeks."

Sterling interrupted, "Dad, what did you do with the money? Please don't tell —"

JR interrupted, "Placed it all on #4 dog in the 3rd race, it's a sure thing—Just Kidding! The good news is that I used it to buy a diamond ring for Katrina if she will have me. I have been lonely a long time and she is such a great friend. I love her very much. Is this okay with you?"

"Yes! Yes! Yes! I think it's wonderful. Call me and tell me what she says. Hey; how are you going to ask her?"

"What do you mean? I'm just going to ask her."

"You can do better than that," replied Sterling.

"When we spoke before you told me she had a love for baseball. Maybe you can get the proposal on the ball field's message board? She likes hiking, how about proposing at the summit of Mount Washington?"

"I get it," replied JR. "I pick up the ring next week, so it gives me some time to plan out the approach."

"I hate to cut this short Sterling, but I am already late for the Gamblers' Anonymous meeting tonight."

"I'm proud of you Dad. Let me know how she answers."

Sarah overheard the conversation. She knew how close Sterling was with his mother, Lynn. Sarah worried that Sterling would be very upset because it was not that long ago that Lynn was murdered.

"Sterling, you OK?" asking in a concerned voice.

"Yes. Yes, I am. Lynn and JR fought over the gambling daily. Their marriage was over years ago. If this mess taught me anything it is to take every day as a gift. If Katrina makes him happy and keeps him out of trouble, I'm all in."

"Great attitude. I couldn't agree more."

Sarah continued, "You need to get the money and the cross, so I can give it to the D.A."

"We need to talk about this. Is there any way I can keep the cross?"

"I don't think so, it belongs to Chapman." Sarah answered with empathy. "I'll ask the D.A. if you could buy it. Maybe Chapman would let you but, even if he did, he would charge you much more than $5500. You did rob his store."

"Also, grab the money, all $2000 that you took out of the safe according to Chapman."

Sterling replied, "Do you want the $2000 or do you want all the money."

"I forgot; you have like $55,000 cash in a bus locker!"

"At the deposition didn't you tell them you had $2,000." asked a very worried Sarah.

"Yes, but the question was 'then you can produce $2,000 and the cross'?"

"I answered 'Yes' because I can. He never asked how much I took. Adding sarcastically, "It's why I try not to give out any extra information."

Continuing, "But seriously, they asked over a hundred questions yet never asked if Sinski asked me what I did with the black bag."

Sarah noted, "Good thing they didn't. That would have been a double click on the pen."

"Can I keep the money?"

"No. It belongs to Chapman."

"Could I use it to bargain for the cross? He's the one that said $2,000."

"No," answered Sarah. "You wanted 'out of this nightmare.' You could face a dozen possible new charges from both the Feds and State. But if we do it right, we might be able to use this to leverage release in the three months rather than six."

"Yes, so worth it." Sterling agreed and left for the bus terminal hoping the cash and cross were still there. The plea deal would be off if they were no longer in the lockers.

Drip.

At the FBI offices.

Chapman had provided the FBI with all the details of the diamond smuggling operation in exchange for witness protection and immunity, but they were unable to build a case connecting Sinski. Pembroke Law did an excellent job in protecting Sinski from any direct communications with the Prosecutors.

All of Chapman's dealings were with Broskavitch, nothing with Sinski himself, the trail ended with Broskavitch.

The FBI investigated many other leads but to no avail.

The clocks were brought into the country by a large jewelry importer. The following shipments were held at US Customs and every item in the shipment was dissected for contraband. Nothing found. Other jewelers that received merchandise from this importer were audited, nothing irregular.

Nothing was found in shipping from the importer to the store. The only oddity was one of the drivers' daughters received a $15,000 scholarship from an unlikely source, but nothing provable.

Chapman's special street people that bought the clocks refused to speak with the Agents. A few days earlier 6 had died from a bad batch of drugs, the rest understood.

Many other individuals that the FBI wanted to speak to just disappeared, including two police detectives.

The FBI had been successful in shutting down this one avenue of diamond smuggling, but they had no case and knew it.

"I just got word from upstairs. They shut us down. I thank you all for your hard work. I know we are all disappointed that we couldn't indict Sinski, but his day will come. Use the rest of the week to put your notes and files away. You new assignments will be given out this Monday. Good luck."

"Hey, Bob (S.A. Clark), what do we do with Chapman. He is still in the safe house." asked one of the agents.

"Put him into witness protection. I heard there is a $50,000 contract on him so put him in as remote a town as possible. Something in Montana sounds nice. He should enjoy that." snickering.

Chapman never made Montana. He was killed within five miles of the safe house.

10 am at D.A. Brooks office.

"Mr. Brooks, you heard Mr. Russell testify at the deposition. You know his motives for burglarizing the jewelry store were to keep his father alive, especially after recently losing his mom." stated Sarah.

"Yes. I do, but a smarter plan would have been to go the police."

"Your right of course, but he was scared. He felt Ned the Knee would do the same thing to his father that had just happened to his mother." replied Sarah.

"I get it and do feel sorry for him and that motive is the main reason I agreed to this settlement with such a light sentence. Three to six months is a bargain, and you know it." said Brooks.

Sarah added, "You know that Chapman lied in court."

"Well it doesn't matter now." replied Brooks.

"You may not have heard but, Chapman was murdered when he left the safe house to start his stay in witness protection. The case against Sinski has been dropped by the Feds. Sinski's group have their tentacles everywhere." he replied.

Sarah needed a moment to process what just happened. With out Chapman's testimony, the entire case was winnable for the defense. Should she ditch the deal and prove Chapman lied about the $2000 and probably the cross value? Chapman told the FBI all the details, could Sarah use that or would it be blocked by the court as inadmissible? At the deposition, Sterling gave all the details of the theft to Brooks. Even though it could not be entered into direct evidence because of the page 3 agreement, Brooks knew all the details meaning where to look to get new proof. How would Sinski react to basically a new trial. Would this put Sterling and even herself more in harm's way with Sinski? What about the money in her bag? No one other than Sterling and herself thinks there is more than $2000. Should she say nothing about the other $53,000?

"Did you bring the cross and money?" Brooks asked.

"Yes, but your case just got a whole bunch weaker. Without Chapman all you really have is the bail issue and no alibi. Without the murder, you can reduce his charge to a misdemeanor, not a felony without a problem. I want him to be successful meaning keeping his certification as a CPA. No one will hire an accountant with a felony charge. The theft was done without threat, force or any weapon: it should be Misdemeanor Unarmed Burglary with three months jail time, then a one-year probation." Sarah pleaded.

"I'm OK with that, but how are you going to sell the Judge."

"How about $53,000." asked Sarah

"A bribe?"

"No. Remember I said Chapman lied. He lied when he told the court $2,000, it was $55,000 in cash Sterling put in the locker."

"I asked Mr. Russell if he had $2,000 at the deposition."

"You asked if he could produce $2000 and he answered yes. No one asked him if he had more."

"Only Sterling and his lawyer, me, knew of this amount until now. He could have kept this money for himself, God knows he could use it. We discussed it last night and his hope was to show the court he is basically an honest person and wanted to do the right thing. His true hope was to reduce the sentence from three to six months to just three months. Reducing the charge is just."

"I won't fight it," said Brooks.

"One last request," asked Sarah.

"The cross was his mother's and means a lot to Sterling. Is there any way he could keep the cross?" asked Sarah.

"Probably, holding the cross in his hands. You could buy it from the estate. The few relatives Chapman had want nothing to do with Chapman or his possessions, only his money. They live in California and are not coming out for services, or anything else. They have hired a firm to liquidate all assets and to probate the estate. That $55,000 will be a pleasant surprise. Here is their card."

"For your ears only, I had the cross appraised yesterday." added Sarah. "Chapman's second lie was that the stones were not real. The cross was appraised at $16,500. It will wipe out all my savings, but I want to buy the cross for Sterling. I will tell him I bought it for $500 like Chapman said. Please keep my secret."

"Sure. You're a good person Sarah."

Judge Cullum asked numerous questions. He grumbled and ranted that they were wasting his and the Court's time. After a stern 5-minute dissertation, including one snort, he raised his gavel and slammed it on the block barking, "SO ORDERED!" as he gave Sarah a one-eyed wink. He also agreed to a 30 day Stay of Execution allowing Sterling time to clean out his apartment and work out some of the divorce issues with Manny, his X.

When Sarah went home, she burst into the room and jumped up into Sterling's arms. Her feet were floating above the floor then wrapped around his legs. She loudly asked, "Who's the best lawyer you know? Who got the sentence reduced to a straight 3 months' time and one-year probation? Who got the charge reduced from Felony Robbery to Misdemeanor Burglary, meaning no loss of your right to practice accounting? Who got you a thirty day Stay before your sentence starts? Who's the best? Say it. Say it loud."

"YOU ARE! I'LL SAY IT AGAIN! YOU ARE." Squeezing her tightly and spinning her in a circle so fast they twirled and fell onto the couch.

"Let's Celebrate." exclaimed Sterling. "Let's go to Ricco's in Wilmington, best Italian food anywhere near. We can get a bottle of wine after for the apartment. And, you are the Best, not just the best lawyer."

"Sounds absolutely fabulous. I'll fill you in on all the details." Sarah said slowly. The adding "While I'm changing, why don't you put away that cot."

Drip.

CHAPTER 24

GETTING READY

Thirty days of freedom felt like an eternity when the words were first spoken to Sterling. In reality, the time went by in a heart beat given all he had to do.

Sarah met individually with both State D.A.'s office and the FBI to finalize and sign all of the paperwork. She then met with the Sheriff's people to find out the specifics of going to jail; i.e. where and when to report, what to wear, what to bring, etc.

Most of the document signings took half a day each due to delays and interruptions. This part of the process was messy, poorly executed, and reminded Sterling of the city Jail.

"Is this what I have to look forward to over the next 3 months. This confusion and lack of discipline is absurd." Sterling told Sarah.

"Sterling remember what I told you. You are strong. You can handle this. Just glance back 3 months and look what it took you to get here. One day at a time.

90 drops to 89, to 88 and before you know it, 1. Think of that song about bottles on the wall."

"Sterling, someone once held a half glass of water in front of me and asked if it was half full or half empty? I told him it was completely full; half with water and half with air, and that both are needed to sustain life. My friend, your cup is overflowing."

Ring... Ring... Ring, Sterling picks up.

"Dad, so nice to hear from you. I never heard back from you. Did you propose to Katrina? Did she say yes? How did you pop the question?"

"I'll answer two of your questions with a question. Will you be my Best Man?"

"I'd be honored, and congratulations. So, give me the details."

"We took a ride up to old Sturbridge Village for the day. I was going to go to Mystic Seaport, but it was too close to the casinos. Anyway, Katrina is a huge history buff. We went through the village, house by house, shop by shop. It was quite interesting to see how people lived a couple hundred years ago, so simple a life but also so hard. No electricity, no refrigerators, no telephones."

"Since we talked, I've been carrying the ring in my pocket; waiting for that special moment to ask and it happened at Sturbridge."

"One of the village members, the blacksmith, made the point that in these days each person needed and depended on each other in the village to survive. The town depended on him, the blacksmith, to reform iron to meet their needs, horseshoes, tools, and the like. He depended on the farmers for food. They depended on the miller, and so on. If your village did not provide you with your needs, you must do without."

"With that speech about needing one another in our minds, we sat at the water wheel that turns the millstones. It was perfect. Katrina looked lovely. Her hair glistened against the afternoon sun's golden reflection in the stream. The green leaves as a background—it was just the right moment. Just the right place and I got back just the right response."

"I don't believe it, my Dad the gambler; a romantic."

"No Sterling, all gamblers are romantics by definition."

"So, when's the date?" asked Sterling.

"It's not set yet, but not for at least three to six months."

"You can go with anytime after the 15th in three months, forget six. I have a lot to fill you in on. I have an amazing lawyer." said Sterling.

Adding, "I will need time; let's see tux, speech, and bachelor party. I have a lot to do. Oh, did I mention a bachelor party?"

Sterling joked about the bachelor party but in truth, it scared him. He not only had he never planned one, he also never even went to one. Sterling would say yes, and then at the last minute find an excuse not to go.

Sterling and JR continued talking for more than an hour.

Just as Sterling hung up the phone it rang again. Sterling jumped, startled. His nose started to bleed.

"Hello!" he almost screamed into the phone.

"Hi, ah, is this Sterling?"

"Yes; sorry, the phone startled me."

"Are you ok?" asked Sarah.

"Yes. Fine. In fact, I just got off the phone with JR my dad. He just got engaged and asked me to be his best man."

"Are you ok with it?" asked Sarah.

"Yes; absolutely, in fact I was wondering if you could dance at his bachelor party for us in your Bow Lake swim wear, without the shorts?" asked Sterling.

"Not in your life."

Sarah and Manny, (Sterling's X), got along quite well. Manny didn't harbor anger towards Sterling, she just no longer loved him, and not sure if she ever had. The three of them met in the old apartment to clean out Sterling's belongings. Manny had all his high-end suits and dress shirts dry cleaned and prepared for storage, just after Sterling was locked out. He took his chess computer, and other objects that meant something special to him, but in truth there were only a few.

Sarah helped Manny get the release on the car and Manny offered to keep the car in storage until Sterling was out of jail, if he wished to buy it back.

Sarah allowed Sterling to store his clothes and the few boxes of belongings in her apartment. She even let him share her bedroom, but not her bed. Still a twin bed against the far wall is better than a cot. Progress.

Sarah was working secretly on trying to buy back the cross from Chapman's estate. The cross was for sale but at now $17,000 she would also need a loan on top of her savings. She bought the cross and put it away for after his release.

CHAPTER 25

PRISON LETTERS

Dear Dad,

Thanks for writing. I'm glad the wedding plans are moving ahead. You asked how prison life was, in your letter.

This prison is nothing like the Boston jail. My section is new. It's ordered, clean and very disciplined. Almost everyone in it is a white-collar criminal.

My cellmate Rob is terrific. On my first day I was greeted with, "Hi, I'm Rob. I occupy the right side of the cell, you have the left. I keep my side tidy and organized and would appreciate you doing the same."

He then offered to teach me how to play chess. Me! Rob is actually very good at the game.

Prison is prison but it's also quite a relief compared to the last few months of my life.

Say Hi to Katrina for me.

Love,
Sterling

Dear Sterling,

I've been working with Manny on the divorce process. She's a love, very helpful and understanding. We're also working on a charity together to help families in Lawrence called Lazarus House. She told me the biggest riff you two had was over wanting children; she did, you didn't. I'm on your side of this argument. My sister has two boys and a girl. Total chaos every day, that's not for me.

With my help, Manny was able to get out of the apartment lease. Lease values have gone way up, so the landlord was more than happy to see you both go. Also, since Manny moved back in with her rich folks, she is very happy. She plans on going back to school and becoming a dentist to join her parent's practice.

With a job, if you stay in my apartment, we can share expenses and you may not have to file for bankruptcy proceedings. A prior bankruptcy would not be a good thing for an accountant's resume.

Speaking of jobs, I have an accounting friend that went to college with me. Both of us were in the Accounting Curriculum for our first two years. I changed to law after but, we remained good friends. If I need an accounting witness for court, I call him. I also send him potential clients. Likewise, if he needs a lawyer, its pro bono. His name is Tom and he has a small firm called Pierce Accounting in Woburn. He has agreed to interview you when you get out. It's not Fine, Fine, and Ginsberg, but at least it's a start and in your field.

I will be up to visit you on Saturday and hope to every Saturday. I was told I can bring up your computer. You won't be allowed online, so no chess, but you may find a use for it.

Miss You,
Sarah

Dear Cmate,

I miss our chess games. I hope prison is treating you well. Say high to Rob for me. He is also good at chess, but I have beaten him.

Hope to connect with you in less than 3 months.

Your Tuesday Chess Partner,
Iwin

Sterling was shocked. Who was this Iwin? How did he know I was in prison, in this prison? How did he know my cellmate? Did Rob tell him about me? Should I confront Rob and ask him directly? The questions kept coming in his mind and kept Sterling up most of the night; just like the night of the theft when he saw in the mirror, he had lost a drop of blood somewhere, but not knowing where.

Drip.

CHAPTER 26

———— ◆ ◆ ————

THE RELEASE

As the prison door opened, Sterling felt a warm flush of freedom. Although it was October, it reminded him of the summer day's he spent with his mother. Even though jail was nowhere near as horrible as he imagined; in fact, he very much liked its clean and orderly structure; it just felt so good to be out!

He felt reborn. A fresh start. The headaches of the past were in the past. His dad's gambling problems seemed under control and headed in the right direction. The divorce was over and behind him. All the connections with organized crime seemed severed. Sterling even almost had a girlfriend. Sarah and he had developed a relationship. As his lawyer, she began to understand the type of person Sterling was; and she approved.

There was a huge smile on both when Sarah stopped the car in front of the gate.

"Get in, get in," yelled Sarah as excited as if she just hit the lottery.

Sterling was just as excited but held it inside. "You look terrific. Thank you so much for picking me up," as he leaned in the window and slowly opened the door.

"Thank you, Sarah, for all your help. If it wasn't for you, I'd still be in jail."

Sterling extended his hand. Sarah grabbed it and pulled him into a strong embrace.

"I'm so glad you're free. Let's celebrate. What's your favorite restaurant?" asked Sarah.

"Newick's."

"Where?"

"Newick's. They have the best lobster pie anywhere."

"Ok," she asked; "give me the directions."

"It is a bit of a ride. It's at Dover Point. Just outside of Portsmouth, New Hampshire. Just below the Maine Bridge."

"New Hampshire? Maine?" exclaimed Sarah.

"Will I need to get an oil change before this trip?" Sarah asked, jokingly.

"It's not THAT far," responded Sterling.

"First we pop up I-91 into Vermont."

"Vermont? Did you say Vermont? Do we cross the Mississippi in this trip? Remember on parole you can't go into Canada!"

"We take 91 north to Vermont, cross over to Route 9 through Keene into Concord; join the first New Hampshire Turnpike to Dover Point. It sounds like a long ride but it's only about two or three hours. It's also a gorgeous ride in early October. The trees are in full fall dress. The reds in Vermont are usually incredible. And I'm so in need of scenery that has no cement or chain link."

"Let's go!" said Sarah. "We'll have supper at Newick's by 7 pm."

Traveling north on Route 91 was just beautiful. The rolling foothills were alive with yellows, reds, oranges with the background of dark pine and evergreens.

Route 9 to Keene was just as beautiful. The road chases a small river that adds to the charm, small waterfalls cascading down ravines; charming old New England towns with white steeple churches; fairs, yard sales. The road was vibrant with activity at every intersection.

"Let's stop in Keene and get a coffee," said Sarah.

"Good idea. And thank you for the road trip," responded Sterling.

"Are you kidding? This is great. I have never taken the time to enjoy New England in the fall. It is wonderful, just wonderful. In addition, I have never heard you talk so much. It's almost like you enjoyed prison."

"Parts of it, I did. Prison was nothing like jail."

While they drank coffee in the bagel shop. "BOOM! BOOM! BOOM!"

"What's that?" Sarah asked the server.

"Homecoming Parade. Football is an important part of our town. Won States last two years. Got a good team this year, might make it three."

"Here's your muffins."

"Can we get them to go?" asked Sterling.

I can package them to go; but you can't go, at least toward Concord until the parade is over, only one road out of town. Go on out and join in on the fun."

And they did. They watched the football players, the cheerleaders, the Pop Warner teams, the parents, cotton candy, popcorn and caramel apples.

The quick stop took over two hours. The leg to Concord was also very heavy with traffic.

"It's too late to make it to Newick's but, were only 30 minutes to the Isinglass Inn. Think John would feed us one of his famous roast beef plates?" asked Sterling.

"I'm gain." replied an excited Sarah.

John remembered them and sat them for a roast beef meal.

"Has anyone caught Bert the bass?" asked Sarah.

"Nothing on the plaque yet."

During dessert, Sarah took out a small jeweler's box and gave it to Sterling.

"I know this meant a lot to you and wanted you to have it."

Puzzled, Sterling opened the box and saw his mother's cross.

"Oh my God, how did you get this? I thought I'd never see it again. This means the world to me. Thank you. Thank you." Beginning to weep.

Larry Cutts

Drip.

The Inn was full, so they drove back to Sarah's apartment. Sarah told him on the ride back that she bought the cross from Chapman's estate for $500.

CHAPTER 27

END GAME

Just as Sterling was leaving his first meeting with his probation officer, a black van with all black tinted windows stopped. The rear door rolled open and the front passenger told Sterling to get in, Mr. Sinski wished to speak with him. Sterling's first instinct was to run, but then he saw Sarah sitting in the van seat wearing large sunglasses. He entered the car.

Put on these eye cups and then the sunglasses. The fewer people that know Mr. Sinski's location, the safer it is for everyone.

Sterling grabbed Sarah's hand and could feel she was shaking terribly, out of fear.

He whispered to Sarah, "It will be alright."

She whispered back, "Are they going to kill us?"

From the front seat came, "BE QUIET, if he wanted you dead it would have happened in prison."

The ride was longer than Sterling expected, or maybe it just seems longer not talking or seeing. He payed attention to the sounds he heard, train crossing bells, low flying aircraft, gravel from a dirt road and more. They were taking them in a manner that purposely confused the directions traveled.

Sterling continued to hold Sarah's hand. She stopped shaking. As the ride lengthened, his mind started to wonder. He tried to picture Derek's office. Dark, full of mahogany and walnut wood tones; few windows if any; a large bar with brass floor rails; maybe even a pool table. Large overstuffed leather couches and chairs placed in the center and large murals of half-naked women to decorate the walls.

The van stopped.

Sarah said to Sterling, "If this is it, I want you to know that I love you deeply."

Sterling gasped. This was the first time Sarah ever said those three words. He answered back, "I love you too."

Although they were both very scared, they were also very relieved because they shared their true feelings that they were both hiding for such a long time.

They were led to a small room and told to remove the eye wear. Just then the double doors opened into Derek's office. The combination of being in total darkness, then bright light temporarily blinded them both. After their eyes adjusted, standing in front of them was Derek Sinski and Mr. Pembroke.

Sterling looked around the office and saw how wrong his image in the car had been. Huge windows overlooked a large swimming pool fenced with evergreens. Steam rose up in a zig zag pattern from the heated water. The room itself was large and very nicely appointed. A small credenza housed two computers with four displays on the wall behind. No Bar nor pool table. Paintings were modern art. In the center of the room there was a small table with two chairs. On top of the table was a large square domed hood?

"Welcome to my home. I believe you both remember Mr. Pembroke."

"Please call me Martin. Sarah so nice to see you again."

"I called this meeting to ask you both a question. You must give your answer considerable thought, but I need your answers before this meeting is over."

"Let me ask Sterling first. I am constantly looking for honest people in my organization. This is especially true for my accountants. I look for honest people in need, usually through no fault of their own, like yourself. You impressed me in the limo. Everything we spoke of was never shared. Again, at the deposition, you proved you are not a risk."

"I am sure you wondered why I would risk so much money to pay your bail. I was testing you to understand your character. There was really no risk of my losing the bail money, my people always knew your location. Our new tracking signals work excellent. Our drone cameras work excellent as well," pointing to a framed picture of Sarah taken from tree height on the beach at the scout camp sunning in her bikini. "Sterling, let me add, you passed your interview."

"Sterling taken aback, "so this is a recruitment?"

"Yes, it is," answered Derek.

"I pay very well, and it comes with a six-figure signing bonus. You also will stay in Boston. I can offer you much, but I know you come as a pair only. Martin, please make your offer to Sarah."

"Sarah, you are a brilliant lawyer. I have never seen such old fashion GUTS as I did when you asked to hire us knowing whom we represent. Your counsel and trial presence are outstanding. Carlson was equally impressed on how you handled the FBI deposition. I want you on my team."

"I can offer a Partnership in the firm with in one year; that alone is worth over a million dollars a year. I'll also throw in a six-figure signing bonus as well."

Derek smiled and said, "We will leave you alone for fifteen minutes, so you can discuss our proposal. We will come back in then for your answer." They left the room.

Sarah looked at Sterling, and Sterling looked at Sarah and they both smiled. Sterling said, "I don't want that life, even with all the perks. I want to work for Tom at Pierce Accounting and I want you."

Sarah hugged Sterling and said, "Me too. I want to run my own company and be my own boss. The offer is tempting, but no."

Although neither one said it, they were both nervous on how Derek might react. He might now see them as a threat.

Derek and Martin came back into the room. Derek asked, "What is your decision?"

"We truly thank you for such a generous offer but are going to refuse." Words not spoken often to Derek or Martin.

Martin slammed his fist on the desk. "I told you she had guts. You just cost me $5,000."

Derek explained, "We made a bet while you talked. I said you would refuse."

Adding, "We are from different worlds. I respect both you and Sarah and wish you well. I hope our worlds do not intersect again in the future, except when we play chess," lifting the square dome. "Iwin has yet to capture Cmate's king, but Cmate has only played on the computer, not facing his opponent."

After an hour, Sterling was winning slightly, then in the next three moves he lost a Knight, a Castle and lastly the Queen.

Derek scowled and said, "Do not lose this game on purpose. I will; be very angry. The win would be meaningless."

Sterling smiled and slid a Pawn on the lower far left of the board exposing his Bishop with a straight diagonal line to Derek's cornered king. "Check and Mate."

Derek grinned, "I have been promoted to a new position in another country, so our rematch will have to be online. Keep your computer on, Tuesday evening."

Spring at Bow Lake

"It's nice to get away. The weekend is supposed to be warm and sunny. I love springtime. Everything is in bloom."

After an early supper at the Inn, they took a walk to the dam. The water was rushing from the lake because of the snow melting off the Mountain Range. The water splashing on the rocks created a small rainbow over the spillway.

They sat on the edge and watched the water explode as it slammed against the rocks in the Isinglass River. It was just beautiful. The setting sun lit up Sarah's hair. All he could think of was his father's description at Sturbridge Village.

"Sarah will you marry me?"

"Yes. Oh yes," as he slipped a diamond ring on her finger with a sparkling diamond.

"But how did you pay for this?"

"I saved for the setting with money earned from work. The stone is special as are my feelings for you. He pulled out his mother's cross; the center stone was missing!

Printed and bound by PG in the USA

USA2019PGIL